Stolen Pieces

A Psychological Crime Thriller

Copyright ©2023 by J.R. Mason
All rights reserved. No part of this publication may be reproduced, stored, or transmitted in any form or by any means without prior written consent from the author.

This is a work of fiction. Any similarities to other events are purely coincidental.

Cover design: J. René Creative
Hands Image: Charles Urban
Editor: J. René Creative

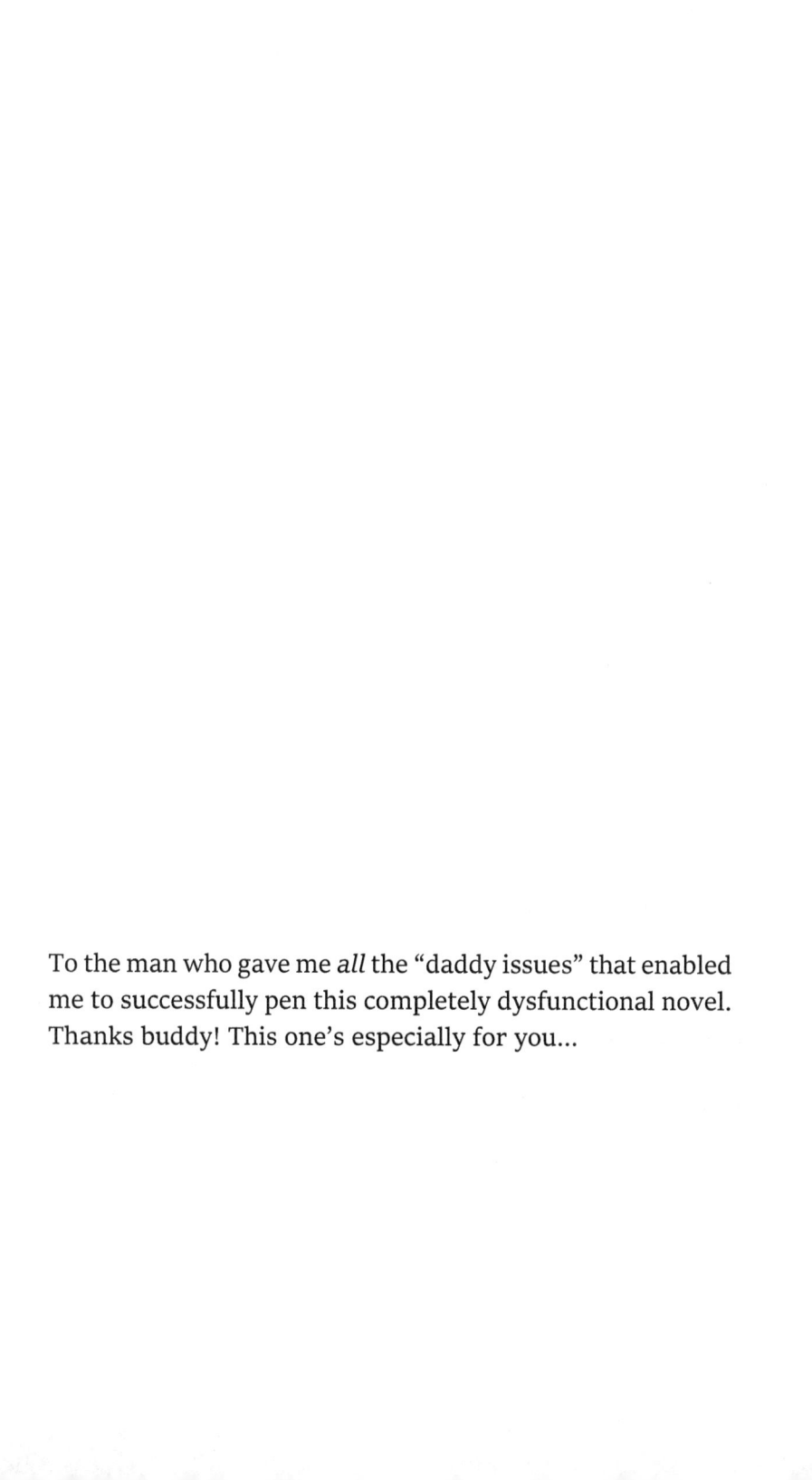

To the man who gave me *all* the "daddy issues" that enabled me to successfully pen this completely dysfunctional novel. Thanks buddy! This one's especially for you...

Content Warnings:

Believe it or not, there is NO GRAPHIC VIOLENCE and NO VIVID DESCRIPTIONS OF DOMESTIC VIOLENCE. However, this book *does* reference Sexual Assault, mentions of Domestic Violence, Strong Language, Child-Related Trauma, Bodily Dismemberment, Sexual Situations, Extramarital Affairs

prologue

Atop fifteen hardwood stairs, a stoic, glassy-eyed little girl stood in a trance-like state, staring blankly at the scene below. Squinting as the sound of static filled her ears, she could see the activity around her, but there was very little coherent sound other than the distinct but distant buzzing of a disconnected landline call.

As thick blood pooled around the base of her mother's head, it began to travel across the landing and absorb into the once clean laundry being brought up the stairs. She watched as her favorite lavender jammies quickly turned a deep shade of red.

Continuing to stand motionless in what seemed like a bad dream, her father frantically pushed her aside, ran down the stairs, and scooped his wife into his arms. His blood-stained hand laid upon her stomach, full with child at just under thirty-two weeks.

The cordless phone at her feet, the little girl continued to stand immobile as she watched a female officer rush up to the second floor toward her in what felt like slow motion. The officer picked her up and carried her down the stairs, shielding her eyes as she stepped over her mother's severely injured body. She watched emptily as EMTs rushed in and moved her father away so they could assess his wife's condition.

In the officer's arms, being swiftly removed from the scene, she could somewhat hear the seemingly confused cries of her father, but the static and ringing in her head overpowered them. Barely able to make out the words spoken around her, she simply watched through the open front door as the EMTs began to take life-saving measures, even though her mother appeared drained of any possible life.

"Sweetheart, can you tell me your name?" asked the female officer with the two long French braids.

Breathing slightly erratically, the trembling child offered no response but continued to stare toward the entryway of the house. She watched from the tail of the ambulance, hopeful that her mother would eventually join her.

"Can you tell me how old you are?" the officer pressed once more.

Another officer positioned himself to block the child's view of the house, so she turned her head away and looked off in the other direction.

"I think she's in shock," the EMT said, placing a hefty but prickly navy blue blanket around her shoulders.

The officer nodded, turning her attention back to the child. "So, your mommy... Did she fall?"

The little girl slowly made direct eye contact with the officer for the first time, staring deep into her empathetic gray eyes and holding that gaze. The officer was silent in hopes that she would actually answer the question, but instead, she simply averted her eyes and stared vacantly out into the distance, shivering in the cold. People were asking questions all around her, but it sounded barely intelligible - like mumbling and dead air. The despondent child sat taking in the scene as red and blue flashing lights illuminated the entire block. Neighbors flooded the area around her home, only kept at bay by one lone officer and a piece of yellow tape.

She tried again, "Did someone *hurt* your mommy?"

Still gazing into the distance, the little girl barely nodded as the cool night wind blew her loose brunette curls across her angelic face. This was the first form of interaction from her the entire evening.

The officer placed her hand on top of the child's to comfort her and asked softly, "Do you know *who* hurt your mommy?"

The trembling youngster surveyed the scene once more, her eyes slowly, intently assessing every person in her field of vision. When they stopped, the officer followed her line of sight, then looked back to the child as one solitary tear strolled down the left side of her lightly freckled face.

"You are such a brave young lady to call us to help your mommy. Wait here, okay? I'll be right back, I promise."

Just as they were rushing the mother to the ambulance on the gurney, officers approached the father who was swiftly tailing them with every intention of riding along to the hospital.

"Miles Evans? We would like you to come with us, please."

"I have to be with my wife," he panted frantically. "I have to go to the hospital with her. And where's my daughter?" he asked, searching the crowd.

"She's safe with our EMTs, but we need you to come with us to answer some questions."

He stood conflicted and unsure of what to do.

"Sir, the sooner we get some information regarding what happened here, the sooner you can get back to your wife," the male officer added.

The second ambulance had already pulled off with lights and the siren engaged, so feeling like he had no other choice, he voluntarily loaded his sweaty body into the back of the police cruiser.

*****

Impatiently pacing the small, gray, nondescript interrogation room, Miles kept watch of the clock. Each tick of every passing second echoed along with his footsteps in the hollow room. Unable to deal with the fact that he was visibly covered in blood, he did his best to avoid observing his 6'5" portly reflection in the enormous, wall-sized, two-way mirror. When he ran his fingers over his full salt and pepper beard, he realized wet blood still lingered throughout his facial hair, which he wiped from his hands onto his light denim jeans. It didn't much matter; they were already ruined.

The two officers who brought him in finally entered the room. "Oh man! How's my wife?" Miles asked desperately.

"I'm sorry to inform you, she's still in critical condition," the female officer replied.

"Shit, I can't do this. I need to get to her," he said as he lunged toward the door.

Blocking his egress, the thin male officer requested, "Mr. Evans, we would *really* like you to have a seat, please."

As his eyes danced back and forth between them, the pair appeared very serious, so Miles hesitantly complied. He slowly ambled over to the metal table while quickly tapping his blood stained fingers against his thigh.

"Okay, so Mr. Evans, can you tell us who all was in your home this evening?"

"Uhhh..." he stammered, seemingly confused by the question. "Me, my wife, and the little one. Why?"

"She's your daughter?"

"Yeah... well, my stepdaughter."

"So, what happened there tonight?"

"What do you mean? I have no idea." The swift nervous tapping then moved from his thigh to the table. "I heard some noise. I- I came 'round the corner... Janet. She... She was on the floor - bleeding." The officers looked at each other skeptically as Mr. Evans began to cry.

"I ran down to her and tried to stop the bleeding but there was so much... I- I couldn't tell where it was comin' from- it was just... everywhere," he said between sobs. "I don't- I don't even know who called! Y'all just showed up! I- I mean, she musta just slipped?"

"Interesting. We have the 9-1-1 call here if you'd like to hear it," the female officer offered, placing a tape recorder on the table in front of him. As she pressed play, Mr. Evans was still tapping his middle finger in rapid succession, anxiously awaiting the audio, staring at the device, then back to the officers.

"9-1-1, what's your emergency?"

"My mommy needs help."

He gasped in response to the small, innocent voice on the recording.

"Okay sweetie, can you tell me your name?"

"Claudia."

"What a beautiful name. How old are you, Claudia?"

"I'll be seven tomorrow."

"And do you know your address, sweetheart?"

"Eight. Oh. Two. One. Five... Kelley Dr."

"Okay Claudia, I'm going to send you help but I need you to stay on the phone with me until they get there, okay?"

"Okaayyy."

"Can you tell me what's going on with your mommy?"

"She's on the floor at the bottom... of the steps with daaaddy."

"Is she awake?"

"Nooo... She's bleeding."

"So, your mommy fell down the steps?"

"Yes... she fell. After daddy pushed her."

"You saw your daddy- "

"Fuck outta here!" Miles screamed and threw the recorder across the room, loudly shattering against the mirror. "I ain't push my wife down them steps! She's havin' my baby, man! She musta slipped, I *told* you!"

"You have quite the temper there, Mr. Evans. *And* it looks as though we've been to your home before on domestic calls," he said, flipping through the pages of his file.

"Are you *serious*!? That was a whole different... This is fuckin' bullshit! Y'all *made* her say that!" he screamed, huffing back and forth across the room, completely enraged. "Wait!" he exclaimed, stopping dead in his tracks. "She said her daddy. Maybe her *real* daddy showed up! I just know it wasn't *me*!"

"She was in *your* home... with just your wife and *you*... by your own admission. Now you're throwing in another father?" the officer replied sarcastically, using air quotes. "Though earlier you said she must've slipped, but you also said you weren't there when she fell, so which is it? 'Cause we all know if you hit her once, you'll hit her again, right? Once an abuser, always an abuser?"

Miles leaned on the table and aggressively stared down at the seated male officer. "Look man, you got *one more time* to say somethin' about me beatin' on my wife."

"Sir, please take a seat," the female officer requested in an effort to diffuse the situation. But her colleague was having none of that and continued to press his buttons.

"You didn't ask about the baby. Is it even yours?" he asked, goading him.

"Muthafucker," he muttered. Before anyone could blink twice, Miles had jumped over the metal table and firmly planted his thick meaty fist into the officer's jaw, knocking him painfully to the floor. A second punch landed, but before he could get a third in, the room quickly filled with officers to physically detain the large man for assaulting one of their own. They may not have been able to arrest him right then for his wife, but that nice little felony charge would at least make sure he'd be held until they could charge him accordingly.

As three officers led him out of the interrogation room and down toward the holding cells, Miles noticed Claudia wrapped in that same blue blanket, seated beside the desk of one of the officers.

"You lyin' little *bitch*!" he shouted as he shook his 300-pound frame free from the officers and took off toward Claudia. She shrieked and jumped into the woman's arms as the other officers hurried to restrain him before he could reach her.

"Why would you *say* that!?" Miles yelled angrily. "Tell them! You know I ain't do this, Claudia! Tell them she slipped!" he screamed while they worked to drag him away as he aggressively maneuvered against them, trying to get back to his stepdaughter.

Once Miles was out of sight and she was calmed down, Claudia remained seated quietly in that chair beside the officer with the French braids, her little legs dangling back and forth. She spent the early hours of her seventh birthday asleep on the station's couch waiting for Children and Youth Services to arrive, only to inform her that her mother had passed away.

STOLEN PIECES

Present day

Of course, the point of therapy was to open up and discuss her innermost feelings, but that wasn't always the easiest thing to do, especially in her line of work where emotional expression could be more of a hindrance than a help. A hush filled the room between the two ladies until a blaring cell phone ring broke the silence, startling them both.

Knowing her phone was supposed to be turned off or on silent, Claudia glanced at the cell, took a deep breath then immediately powered it down.

"Your stepfather again?"

"Miles actually," Claudia immediately corrected. "Just Miles. And how could you possibly know it was him?"

"I'm sorry. *Miles.* Because during the short time we've been working together, I've noticed the smallest micro expressions anytime he's the topic of discussion. Your nose does this slight twitch every time he's mentioned," she explained, imitating the twitch.

Dr. Sydney Pearce was so incredibly observant and could already point out many idiosyncrasies of which

Claudia was strangely unaware. The ability to assess everyone else in a room was Claudia's forté, however, her own self-reflection and assessment needed work. She felt as though many things about her could actually use some adjustment. The only plus side about feeling that way was that at least she was able to acknowledge those things and seek help. Dr. Pearce was just who she needed.

They became acquainted after a particularly difficult case a little over a month ago. Claudia and her partner were following up on a lead in a homicide investigation when on the way to the car, they heard fighting, glass breaking, and a little girl crying in one of the neighboring homes. Upon their arrival, the scene had quieted, but they knocked to do the welfare check anyway. The woman who answered the door appeared to be fine physically and said that she and her husband had been having a slight verbal disagreement. As they discussed the particulars, an adorable raven-haired child, who looked to be about four, clung to her mother's leg as she ran her fingers through the child's thick straight hair, seemingly out of habit and affection. That made Claudia smile, remembering how her mother used to play with her curls.

There were no charges to be pressed, so the detectives left the scene and wrote up the incident accordingly.

Less than 72 hours later, everyone was back at the residence to investigate the shooting deaths of that mother and daughter, while the father feigned ignorance and claimed innocence. When the victims were taken by the coroner, it was revealed that the mother's body was covered in bruises, all in various stages of healing. She had been physically abused regularly for a length of time, which would've been obvious had she not been fully covered during Claudia's first visit.

The idea that she looked into the eyes of that little girl and did not protect her crushed Claudia's soul. She had half expected a gruesome scene, but what they found was the little girl in a princess-themed bedroom. She was lying peacefully in her bed with her mother beside her in a fetal position holding a book. She must've simply fallen asleep reading to her daughter, much like Claudia recalled her mother doing with her. No other scene had affected her in such a way that she had to step out.

Once she was far enough away from the crime scene, for the first time ever, Claudia broke down. Bent over with her hands on her knees for support, tears flowed more freely than they ever had in her entire adult life. Hyperventilating, barely able to catch her breath, a kind, curvy, dark-brown-skinned woman with shoulder-length curly dreadlocks hurried from her home to check on her. As Claudia straightened up, the woman took notice of the badge and gun on her hip, recognizing her as a detective. She didn't know what specifically had happened, but for someone who saw violence and death on a daily basis to have such an emotionally painful reaction, it must have been pretty awful. She offered her comfort and a business card to come to see her if she ever needed to talk.

That weekend, when Claudia emptied her pants pockets to throw a load in the washer, she came across the card and called the next day to schedule the therapy appointment. It had been a while since she had seen a good mental health professional.

After her mother died tragically the night of her fall and her stepfather, the only other parent she'd ever known, was arrested and subsequently charged with aggravated assault and homicide, Claudia was placed in foster care. The Jacobs family was kind to her and she even got a big sister out of the deal when she was later adopted by them. Of course, initially the new parents were nervous that their only child would have issues with a much younger sibling coming into the picture, but Claudia and her foster sister, Hope, got along famously and became exceedingly close, despite their nine-year age difference. Hope even gave Claudia a cute nickname that only *she* could call her.

The Jacobs family knew that taking in a young child who had witnessed a horrific parental death could be a challenge, so it was decided that therapy would likely be necessary to help her cope. But she seemed to be doing so well in her new environment that they didn't prioritize it. However, the death of the family dog expedited that process. Both girls were extremely attached to the four-year-old Rottweiler, Rico. One morning on the way out to catch the bus for school, Claudia opened the door to find Rico on the porch foaming at the mouth and struggling to breathe. It appeared as though he had been poisoned, presumably by the neighbor a few doors down who didn't care for animals on or near his property. He especially wasn't fond of their large vicious-looking pet who was really a giant teddy bear and so incredibly gentle with the children. There was nothing they could do about it though, because they had no proof.

Claudia melted down after seeing yet *another* death, so they immediately found a good child psychologist to assist.

Once Miles Evans was finally convicted and sentenced for the death of his wife, the well-connected inmate somehow managed to find out where Claudia was and would call regularly from the prison. The family changed phone numbers multiple times over the years, but with his many associates on the outside, he somehow still managed to obtain their contact information. The calls finally stopped for a long while after Hope, not knowing any better, answered the phone and accepted the charges for the collect call. Thinking it was Claudia on the phone, Miles yelled, swore, and threatened her. He ended up having his phone privileges temporarily suspended, then subsequently fully monitored, after the Jacobs' filed a police report. Since all phone calls are recorded, they were able to listen as a grown man made appalling threats toward an innocent child.

So far, Dr. Pearce was incredibly easy to talk to. It was effortless to share with her the fact that her family seemed to be the root of almost all of her issues. But despite those many setbacks, Claudia somehow managed to stay fairly well-composed through it all. Whether she was really that tough, or just putting on a stellar façade, she managed to stay focused and continue into her chosen field of law enforcement.

"Last time we ended our session, you mentioned that Miles was the reason you wanted to be a police officer?" Dr. Pearce inquired. "How so?"

"I don't remember everything from that night, but I *do* remember all the first responders."

Claudia had immediately noticed how they all came together to her aid and tried so diligently to help her mom. They were all so caring, but they were also mostly men.

"There was only one female officer on the scene. I still remember her braided hair," she paused. "She made me feel like everything would be okay. After everything that happened with Miles and my mom... I- there just should've been more women around."

What about the other small children like her who were scared and needed the warmth and tenderness of a maternal-like figure? Claudia longed to be able to provide that, in addition to showing little girls that they could be anything they wanted to be - even if it was a detective in a male-dominated profession.

"I just wanna help people and provide a level of safety that I didn't feel growing up watching my mother being snatched and thrown around by her husband." She took a deep breath, "But now I'm starting to question everything. I should've done more to protect that family. I should've pressed the charges my*self*!"

"But on what grounds? You said that everyone appeared okay. You did what you could in that moment, and what happened wasn't *your* fault. But if you're going to continue to *blame* yourself, you have to figure out a way to *forgive* yourself."

Claudia nodded and stared out the window that overlooked the Allegheny River, wondering why some of it was green and other patches of it were brown. Then she wondered what ever made her think it was okay to engage in water sports in that cesspool.

"Tell me about the bad dreams. Are you still having them?"

"Not every night, but yes."

"Have you tried the sleeping meds I suggested?"

"Yeah, they just put me to sleep faster, so the nightmares come sooner," she replied sarcastically.

Dr. Pearce sighed with a defeated smile, revealing the gap between her teeth, "I never thought of it that way."

Claudia smiled back, "Yeah, me either."

"I'm going to give you some visualization exercises to try before bed to see if that helps any."

Claudia nodded skeptically, still worried that no exercise, technique, or drug could overpower the horrors that awaited her every time her eyes closed.

2

Claudia held her breath when she heard the creaking of the old wooden floor. Someone was definitely in her house... creeping slowly down the hall. She watched in terror as the doorknob to her bedroom slowly turned, and someone entered. Unable to see the intruder's face or upper body, his top half was obscured by the covers she peered out from beneath. All that was visible were his jeans and work boots covered in the dried mud that he inconsiderately tracked through her house. Her heart raced as he slowly approached the bed and forcefully grabbed her. Before she could scream, Claudia jolted herself upright in the bed wheezing, trying to catch her breath.

She would always wake up in a cold sweat, scared to death from the same two dreams that had been haunting her for years. They were the primary reasons she locked her bedroom door at night, even though she lived alone.

With her bed sheets and skin damp to the touch, she ran her sweaty fingers through her hair and tugged on it growling in exasperation that she continued to have these night terrors. Being alone only made it that much worse.

She placed one hand over her chest and the other on her stomach taking deep breaths to try to steady herself and lower her heart rate.

As a trained professional who carried a gun for a living, she would announce herself as law enforcement, even though she wasn't required to, then pump him full of lead in a hot second. But for whatever reason, Claudia couldn't figure out why in these dreams she was always paralyzed with fear and unable to access her firearm to defend herself.

Finally, a little more composed, she reached over for the glass of water on her nightstand and noticed that it was 5:30 a.m. At least she wouldn't need her alarm.

As she stood up, the outdoor motion sensor light suddenly turned on, which startled her, causing the glass to slip from her hand and shatter around her bare feet.

"Damn it!" she hissed. That was the third glass she had broken this year for the same reason. Though she didn't actually think she needed it, Claudia quietly pulled her gun out of the nightstand. Her nerves were already frazzled from that nightmare, but adding the motion sensor lights to that didn't help.

Stepping over the shards of glass and puddle of lukewarm water, she tiptoed to the window. Her heart thudded in her ears as she peeked through the side of the curtain. Claudia didn't disclose this because she didn't want Dr. Pearce to add "paranoia" to her laundry list of issues, but she couldn't help but feel like someone was watching her. She wasn't able to confirm this, nor had she actually noticed anyone following her. And the idea that anyone would be out here on her property was so implausible. She lived in a rural area where there wasn't another house for at least a half mile. So as she stood scrutinizing the brightly illuminated area outside of her house, all she could dwell on was the fact that her therapist would think she was nuts. But that didn't change the fact that she felt someone's eyes on her... often.

When she detected the two deer prancing down the back steps of her deck, Claudia released the breath she had been holding and put the firearm away.

"They better not have been mating on my deck! *I* haven't even gotten to mate on my deck yet!" she grumbled as she cleaned up the broken glass at her bedside.

*****

In what would appear to be a large cable car, akin to a New Orleans streetcar gliding up the side of a massive mountain, the two Monongahela inclines transported commuters from Station Square 400 feet up to Mount Washington and back. While many would use it as a mode of transportation to work in the city, others would simply take the ride for enjoyment. Tourists delighted in snapping pictures at the lookout because the geometric silhouette of Downtown Pittsburgh acted as a breathtaking backdrop, whereas many locals opted to take advantage of that environment for marriage proposal opportunities.

Another spectacular focal point from that altitude was Point State Park, where the two main rivers converged to form an even larger body flowing from North Side all the way to the Mississippi River. From that elevation, spectators could fully visualize why The Point, as it was affectionately called, was the heart of Pittsburgh. From that site extending through the remainder of the city limits, over 400 bridges and tunnels were like arteries and veins pumping drivers and pedestrians in and out of town. The constant flow of movement made the Steel City feel like a beautiful living entity.

"Ever wonder what would happen if the brakes went on one of these things? You think there's something at the bottom to help stop us from crashing into the street below?" a fellow rider could be easily overheard asking his friend.

With wide eyes, a mother diverted her attention from her book to see who would ask such a question in a small claustrophobic space, clearly unaware of what little ears may also be listening. She looked to her small child, but he seemed oblivious to the conversation at hand, as the car began its four-minute ascent up the steep track.

"Your son is adorable," the male rider seated across from her commented, seemingly to provide a distraction from what they had clearly both just heard.

"Oh, thank you so much. He's such a mess," the mother commented with a warm smile as she tousled his hair. "Say thank you to the nice man," she requested.

The adorable freckle-faced five-year-old, who was covered in powdered sugar from the donut he was eating, looked to his mother, then to the stranger, and shyly offered a thank you as he continued consuming his breakfast pastry.

With powdered sticky fingers, the child tugged on his mom's shirt to get her attention. While still engrossed in her book, she asked, "What's wrong?"

He leaned in closer to her and whispered, "Mommy, that man has three feet."

Still reading, she replied, "Sweetie, you know people only have two feet."

He continued to stare across the small enclosed space in confusion. "But Mommy, this one has *three!*" he pressed with greater concern.

"Just finish your donut, baby. We're almost at the top."

"But Mommmmy…" He placed the remainder of his donut on the germ-infested wooden public transportation seat and stood up beside his mother to get her full attention. As she again diverted her concentration from her book to tell her child that we don't stand on seats, she noticed the look of panic on his face. She followed his gaze across the incline car, where it definitely appeared that the man who just complimented her son's appearance did, in fact, have more than two feet. Directly beside this passenger's two feet lay a simple gray and white Adidas tennis shoe.

"Oh baby, it's okay. Someone just left their shoe on the incline. It's a little weird, but it happens sometimes." She offered that explanation knowing that it really wasn't a common occurrence, but if it would stop the barrage of questions so she could make it through just one page of her book uninterrupted, she'd say just about anything.

"But won't his foot be cold?" he asked with genuine concern.

"You know what?" she said, closing her book in defeat, "It might just be. When we get to the top, we can take it to the lost and found and maybe he'll come back for it. Okay?" She smiled.

That answer seemed to satiate him. No one tells parents how much work it will be and how many weird things they will have to say or do in order to teach their children to be good human beings. Touching a dirty shoe left on public transportation was just a sacrifice she was willing to make that morning to instill those morals.

"Sir, excuse me again. That shoe that's beside you…"

The gentleman glanced down and could see the front of the shoe and some of the laces poking out, so he used his foot to scoot the shoe completely from under his seat. As he did so, he violently jumped up while trying to move away, inadvertently knocking himself into other nearby riders. The physical commotion shook the rickety box on the track which startled the passengers even more. Screams and disorientation took over the enclosed space when it became clear there was still a foot in that shoe.

"Holy shit is that real?!" a young man screamed as he opened his phone.

They thought he was going to call 9-1-1, but he instead snapped a selfie in front of it and began to record a TikTok.

The mother shook her head as she called for assistance.

"9-1-1, what's your emergency?"

"Good morning, We're on the Mon incline in the car going up and... well, there's a foot in here. Like a *human* foot..."

"Ma'am, could this possibly be a prank?"

"If it is, it's not very funny."

After three consecutive hellish nights of broken sleep, there was no way Claudia was making it through the day without a serious caffeine fix. Just as she was approaching the shop, her partner, Lainey, was hopping out of her vehicle with similar caffeine-related intentions. Fortunately, they were able to pretty much walk right up to the counter, having missed the early a.m. rush.

"Good morning, what can I get you today?" asked the thin, flamboyant cashier with long white-boy dreadlocks.

"I'll have a Venti S'mores Frappuccino," Lainey requested.

"Hi. Ma'am. Do you see the sign back there?" He waved his arm dramatically behind him. "You are in The Steamy Bean Coffee Shop. We ain't Starbucks. You can order your coffee here like a *normal* human - in English, please. Now, what can I get you?"

Lainey and Claudia exchanged looks as Claudia just shrugged her shoulders and smirked.

"Fine. I will have a *large* S'mores Frappuccino, please. Oooh, can I get extra marshmallows on top?"

"Extra marshmallows? What are you, five?" Claudia ribbed.

"Excuse me, umm aren't you the same person who ate a bunch of them out of my *last* frap? So it's a good thing I got extra."

When Lainey pulled her card out to tap it on the machine to pay, Claudia noticed the name on it.

"Your name is Elaine? How did I not know that?"

"Yes," she whined, rolling her eyes. "It's my most shameful but best-kept secret," she snickered. "Why would my parents name me Elaine Crane? Like, who does that to their child?"

Claudia chuckled, even though she knew she shouldn't, but she couldn't help it. During their entire ten months together, she only knew her new partner as Detective Lainey Crane. The 5'7" blonde with breasts so perky they couldn't possibly be real, looked way more like a "Lainey" to her.

"If my partner and I ever have children, we have made a solemn vow to never give them names that rhyme."

"And for you, ma'am?" the cashier asked.

Before Claudia could respond, she heard a light tenor voice correct him, "It's *detective*. And she'll have the medium caramel toffee iced latte with extra whip. Here you go," he said, setting it on the counter.

With raised eyebrows, Lainey looked at Claudia, who shifted her eyes to the ground. The cashier delivered a similar look to his barista, Levar.

"Oookayyy then... That'll be-"

"On the house," Levar interrupted the cashier.

Still avoiding eye contact with Lainey, Claudia looked at Levar offering a shy smile, and mouthed the words, thank you.

Poor, sweet Levar. He had the biggest crush on Claudia but was nowhere near self-aware enough to realize how out of his league she was.

Standing at about 5'11" with smooth, creamy, dark chocolate skin and perfect white teeth, Levar *could* be pretty handsome if he had any idea what to *do* with himself. He hid soft brown eyes behind a pair of the thickest glasses imaginable and his personal style left much to be desired. This young man almost never wore pants long enough to reach their intended destination. So his standard white crew socks that extend up to mid-calf were always visible and even more noticeable on days when his attire dictated that they should be black.

Interacting with Levar always made Claudia think of the movie *She's All That* - the one where the girl gets made over even though she was never actually ugly in the first place. He simply needed a stylish, beguiling male role model to take him under his wing and give him a makeover and a slight personality overhaul.

Anyone paying attention could tell that Levar didn't have much experience with dating or interacting with women. He seemed too eager and like someone who could be easily manipulated. Yet somehow, even though he wore the same clunky, plain, white tennis shoes Claudia's grandfather used to wear, he still somehow possessed all the nervous confidence in the world when it came to asking her out.

With those few minor adjustments, Levar might be a great catch for some other woman. But at only twenty-six years old, he was much too young for Claudia who was nine years his senior.

He had asked her out a few times when they first met and she never quite answered, but merely changed the subject. That didn't stop him from having her very specific coffee and pastry order memorized. A few times there had been a line to order, but by the time she made it to the cash register, he would already have her order completed and ready. Like he could somehow always spot her in the crowd. It was flattering.

He sent her a follow request on Instagram which she considered declining, but he seemed like a sweet enough guy. She was going to see him a few times a week at the shop anyhow, so she just approved it. She didn't really post too often anyway - just random creative meals she would eat, her pets, and a few vacation pictures, but only after she had returned.

Levar tried diligently to be a gentleman and not to stare at Claudia's hind quarters as the two ladies exited the cafe, but try as he might, he just couldn't help it. "She's gonna go out with me one day, man. Watch."

The cashier snickered in an effort to contain his laughter. "You could offer her fine ass all the coffee in Columbia, that woman is *not* going out with you."

"So what was that about?" Lainey questioned as the door swung closed behind them.

"What do you mean?" Claudia asked obtusely.

"Since when are you shy? And how aren't you hot with all those clothes on?"

"Leave me alone; I'm comfy. And hey! I *am* shy," she laughed.

"Oh okayyy," Lainey teased sarcastically as they strolled a few doors down to work.

"So, whose bright idea was it to put a coffee shop this close to the station?" Claudia complained. "I'm gonna go broke."

"Well, I think it's a great idea! The city knew what they were doing because we need access to caffeine to stay awake," Lainey chuckled. "We got criiiime to stop! Killas to catch!" she joked, posing in a superhero stance with coffee as her weapon of choice. Lainey was a wild one to work with. Uber professional when she needed to be, but outside of that, she was a total goofball.

"You mean, 'weight to gain' with all these extra calories," Claudia said, patting her stomach.

"Well if you would just order normal coffee and stop drinking dessert in a cup, that would be a non-issue."

Oh, you're one to talk with your liquid s'mores for breakfast," Claudia teased as she dramatically took a long sip of her highly caffeinated liquid diabetes.

"Hey Teddy," they both said in unison to the stocky officer who often worked the front desk at the precinct.

"Ladiiies!" he said with a full grin and round reddish cheeks. "Where's *my* coffee?"

"Next time," Claudia shouted back with a big smile as they entered the elevator.

"Two sugars, one cream! Holdin' ya to it," he shouted back happily as the doors closed.

"Hey, have you peeped that new detective?" Lainey asked as they stepped off the elevator and sauntered to their adjoining desks. Glancing up and over Claudia's shoulder at the tall, well-built specimen, "He's a rookie, maybe a little young, but definitely not bad."

Claudia was just about to turn and look, "Wait, wait!" Lainey interrupted. "Not yet... Hold on... Okay now!"

Glancing over her left shoulder, Claudia accidentally locked eyes with the young newbie. She had already met him, but decided to play dumb.

"You're terrible at this. I thought you said the coast was clear," Claudia grumbled.

"It was! But did you feel it? Was there some heat when you made eye contact? Because you need a man; it's been a good minute. I mean it's not like you can find one out in the field."

Lainey was not wrong. Yes, the rookie was quite easy on the eyes, clean cut with a baby face, dirty blond hair, a hazel gaze, and a great smile. But he looked like he just walked across the high school stage and shook hands with the principal to receive his diploma. Usually not her type. She preferred her men a little older, more skillful, and a lot more rugged. Now his more experienced partner with the full, jet-black beard and bald head, Eric Burgess? He could punch her ticket. Twice.

Lainey was also correct that she probably could use a steady committed man in her life. It had been just over a year since her split from Scott. As they were preparing for an evening out, his phone pinged with an incoming message alert. As she picked it up to walk it to him in the bathroom, a selfie of a beautiful bleach-blonde woman materialized on the screen. In the background, which was probably the true intent of the photo, was Scott gently kissing the forehead of a brand new infant swaddled in blue. He tried to lie his way out of it - to a detective who detects lies for a living. After three years of dating, Claudia knew that he was an only child, so there was no possible way that the baby was his nephew, as he vehemently proclaimed. This man she intended to marry at some point and start a family of their own, had a baby with another woman and didn't plan to tell her. What was the strategy? To live a double life until he got caught?

Though she was trying to talk it out in therapy, it was taking Claudia a little longer to recover from that deception than she had hoped. Trust issues don't simply dissipate overnight when someone has been wronged to that magnitude. So she was content having casual relationships for the time being. No one could hurt her if she didn't actually care.

"Lane, can my love life wait until *after* work?" Claudia asked with a sigh as she opened her laptop. Patiently sipping on her morning beverage and waiting for the PC to boot, Claudia slowly took in the busy happenings of the squad room. All seemed normal until something unexpected caught her eye.

She politely excused herself, as she swiftly ejected from her seat. Trying to be as nonchalant as possible, the detective quick-stepped across the room, then through the double doors. She slowed her pace looking around the eerily empty hallway.

He's here. I know I saw him. Claudia slowed her breathing to listen more closely until that breath was taken away as she was abruptly snatched by her arm and dragged into the hallway stairwell.

Panting heavily, she drew her weapon and took aim.

"*Hey hey hey hey*! It's just me! I'm sorry don't shoot," he said with his hands up and open in a submissive position.

"Are you fucking crazy!? I could've *killed* you!" she panted. "Why would you do that!?"

"I'm sorry, I just wanted to surprise you."

"Roses are a nice surprise," Claudia vented as she secured her .40 caliber Glock back into its holster. "An edible arrangement. A trip to Cabo, perhaps. Hiding like a creeper in a stairwell grabbing unsuspecting women in the night? Your woo'ing needs work."

"Into the night though? Really, Claudy? It's 9 a.m. But hey, you have *your* caffeinated way of waking up, and I have mine. Scaring the hell out of the most beautiful, badass, heavily-armed woman I know is like a straight shot of adrenaline. I like to live on the edge," he teased, as he inserted his index finger into the waistline of her well-fitted jeans and pulled her closer to him and into the corner of the concrete emergency stairwell.

He ran his large hands down her waist and around the corner until they were full of Claudia's round cheeks, pulling her hips against his until there was no more space between them.

"Fine. You're forgiven," she sneered while they gazed into each other's eyes as she played with the dark curly hair at the nape of his neck. She closed her eyes as he slowly leaned in toward her and grazed his smooth lips across her forehead. He planted a soft kiss there before moving down to the tip of her nose and leaving one there as well. She tilted her head back so that her lips would meet his and they engaged in a most passionate and flavorful embrace.

There was always so much heat and tension between the two of them. Anytime he would be on-site to discuss a case with her squad, as his eyes panned the room while he spoke, they always lingered on her for a few additional seconds before moving on to the next person. It was work to play it cool considering his intense gaze alone altered her breathing patterns. Claudia always felt like their attraction to one another was palpable, but Lainey, who was constantly in her business, never said anything. So maybe it was just her own internal sexual struggle, which was good. This was not something that ever needed to be made public.

They jumped apart at the sound of the door above opening and closing. Breathing halted as they listened intently to the footsteps of the people who sounded like they were going up the steps, so they were finally able to exhale.

"See, this wasn't such a bad surprise," he whispered as he began to walk down the stairs toward the main exit. "And even better, since you don't ever wear lipstick, we don't have any cleanup." He winked at her and she smirked as she turned to make her way back to her desk.

"You kinda rushed outta here. Is everything okay?" Lainey asked, pulling her long straight tresses up into a neat high ponytail.

"Yep," Claudia replied, avoiding eye contact ready to retake her seat.

"That's good because the captain wants to see us. I think they found another," Lainey sighed as they made their way across the squad room.

"Detectives!" Captain Edward Higgins yelled as they entered his office. "Can either of you tell me what the *hell* is happening in my beautiful city!?" While it was definitely a rhetorical question, it was valid. "We have another incident, this time down at Station Square on the inclines. There are already officers on the scene from the 9-1-1 call."

"You mean the same as the-"

"Yesss!" the handsome, gray-haired, slender man exclaimed while he shoved three more pieces of Nicorette gum into his mouth. Trying to quit smoking had been hell on him and every other employee in the building.

"I don't get it. What kind of sick bastard has time to leave *feet*? Like, *just* feet in my city!? Go do the thing. Get me the witnesses. I want the camera footage. Find the person leaving the fucking *feet*!" he yelled, while he slapped a NicoDerm patch onto his arm. "Excuse my French," he blurted out.

The two detectives looked at each other on the way out of Captain Higgins' office. "I'm gonna need a *real* drink. I can't believe this is happening again," Lainey continued as they walked over to her desk to grab the keys.

4

Claudia and Lainey arrived on the scene to find officers speaking to multiple witnesses. Both inclines were shut down temporarily as officers and crime scene investigators swarmed the location lifting prints and photographing the scene from every possible angle. News crews began arriving to troll for information to report, but they were nowhere near ready to discuss this publicly.

"Detectives Martinez... Crane," an officer nodded. "Medical Examiner's in there already."

The detectives nodded back as they rounded the corner and entered the incline car to find the M.E., Dr. Alessandra Berardi, wearing trendy wire-rim glasses and black nitrile gloves, kneeled down examining the foot.

Without even looking up, "Good morning, detectives."

"Clearly not for the owner of that foot," Lainey replied.

Dr. Berardi looked up at her over her stylish eyewear. The comment was tacky, but not untrue. "This time it's a right foot."

"So this could belong to the owner of the left foot from a few weeks ago in Schenley Park?"

"It could. They appear to be sawed off at a similar location. That foot was a size eleven. I'll be able to tell you a definitive size once I get this to the lab – it's not on the bottom of this shoe. And of course I'll have them run DNA to see if it matches."

Claudia nodded. "Well, hopefully it does. Otherwise, that means we're looking for another victim, which means possibly a serial."

"Oh man, the captain will *not* like that," Lainey grumbled.

I've heard he's trying to quit smoking," Alessandra replied abruptly while placing the body part in a clear evidence container. "I don't think there's enough gum and patches in Pittsburgh for him to take that information well. Best of luck," she remarked as she brushed past them toward Grandview Avenue where her white Audi SQ8 was parked. Under normal circumstances, she would be driving the official van, but she got the call on the way in to the lab.

Lainey looked to Claudia, "Maybe it's just me, but I don't feel like the city pays me enough to carry body parts not attached to a living person in my new Audi SUV."

"Please, they don't pay you enough to *drive* an Audi like hers," Claudia replied as she visually examined the incline car. "That well-hidden camera up on the right points down in this direction. The other one on the bottom left should show the door. We need that footage."

Rookie detective, Tanner Lockhart, escorted the incline operator to the scene.

"Hello, Mr.-"

"Wilkes. Jake Wilkes."

"Mr. Wilkes, I'm Detective Claudia Martinez and this is Detective Lainey Crane. What can you tell us about these cameras? Do they provide a live feed? Or is it simply recorded and lives somewhere else?"

"I have a live feed in the booth with me, but like I told the other officers, these cameras have been down for the past couple a days."

"In both cars?"

"And in the waiting area below. The cameras in the other car came back online late last night."

"So maybe we can see into this car from that camera?"

"No, the way the inclines work, it's a pulley system - they have to balance each other out, so if one is at the top, the other is at the bottom."

"So they're never at the same place at the same time except when they pass each other in the middle?"

"Yes ma'am. And it's quick – only about two seconds."

"So if the cameras were down, how would you know to open the doors at the bottom, if you're at the top?"

"There's a buzzer down there. I can open the doors to allow passengers to enter. Then it makes an announcement that the doors will close. Just gotta hope they have enough sense to not be in the way, I guess."

"I still want the footage from the other car just in case," she said to Detective Lockhart. "And get me the person who worked this thing last night. I need to know if he or she had a buzz and brought up an empty car. That could help give us a timeline."

"I'll contact Port Authority," he replied stepping away.

"Thank you for your help, sir. Here's my card if you think of anything else."

*****

Back at the station, detectives were working to pull up the video from the second incline car.

"Port Authority's being a little sketchy over there," Lockhart remarked. "They don't want any blowback, I guess, because they took their time getting those cameras operational again."

"Did they say anything else?"

"Just that the cameras were new additions to the incline cars since that three-month renovation took place. They've been experiencing some glitches but can usually get them back online in a reasonable amount of time. This time they went down for hours. Our people are checking the electrical lines to see if maybe someone intentionally tampered with them."

"Hmm, that wouldn't totally shock me," Claudia remarked. "What are the odds that someone would leave human remains in a public location and the cameras just *happened* to be out of commission? That would be too coincidental."

"So you're thinking it had to be someone who *knew* the cameras were down or took them down?" asked Captain Higgins as he unconsciously picked at the edges of the patch on his arm.

"Exactly. One of those cameras faces the entrance, and that foot was left beneath the seat just to the left of that door. So had that camera been operational, our delivery person's face would have been on it," Lainey confirmed pounding her fist on the desk she was leaning over.

They re-watched the footage from the beginning several times.

"Okay, so the inclines are down and locked for about four and a half hours each night. They start running at 5:30 a.m. and can hold up to twenty-three people in each car," Claudia pointed out. "The left car, where the foot was found, was empty on the way up, while passengers rode the right side down. They remained docked for a few minutes to load passengers, then started running again and passed each other in the middle." The group continued studying the footage to see if they could notice anything happening in the few seconds of video that was visible into the other car each time they'd pass one another, but nothing looked especially suspicious.

"This isn't helpful. We have no way of knowing if a passenger made the drop that morning because the cars were so full," Lainey said, pacing the aisle between the clusters of desks. "It's very well possible that the foot had already been there from the night before when the incline closed and no one noticed it in the morning because there was standing room only."

"Right, so the area under the seat wouldn't be visible to anyone until there were fewer people in the car making the floor area visible to anyone seated," Claudia confirmed.

"So what about the other foot in the park last week?" Lockhart asked. "Could that give us any clues?"

"The owner of that foot was Clem Rossi."

"Wait, Rossi," another detective questioned. "Why does that name sound so familiar?"

Claudia felt all of the blood rush from her face and her stomach twist, "He's the one who killed his wife and daughter last month."

"Allegedly," someone interjected, but she didn't care to acknowledge who.

"Fine," Claudia interrupted. "*Allegedly* killed his family." That image of them cozy in bed reading with a single gunshot wound to each of their heads was emblazoned in her mind. She clenched her fists, intentionally digging her nails into her palms to fight back the emotional pain and impending tears.

"Okay, so he didn't jump bail or skip town as originally thought."

"He's not jumping or skipping anywhere without a- never mind..." Lockhart joked but realized it was inappropriate.

Claudia sighed heavily, but it wasn't nearly enough to assuage her nausea and grief. "Heading over to the M.E.'s office – I need some air," she announced as she stood up from her desk and grabbed her keys. "Will keep you posted."

Lainey retrieved her jacket and swiftly followed Claudia out the door.

*****

Just as Alessandra was grabbing her oversized Louis Vuitton bag to head out, Claudia and Lainey stormed through the metal double doors into her autopsy suite.

They were always amazed by the clean smell of the room. The first time Claudia visited, she expected the foul aroma of death, but instead, she was met with the scent of cleaning products, which was quite pleasant when compared to the alternative.

"Well as usual, your timing *could* be better," she said with sass as she turned to put her purse back down.

Lainey smirked at Claudia, who immediately rolled her eyes but quickly plastered a fake smile on her face before Alessandra turned back around.

"Meeting my husband for lunch, but he can wait," she remarked emotionlessly as she donned a new pair of black gloves and retrieved the bare decomposing foot from the cooler.

"Thank you."

"So. I've got some good news and some bad news," Alessandra explained. "Or maybe it's bad news and worse news. The first foot that was found was a size eleven. This one is a size twelve."

"Damn it," Claudia muttered under her breath.

"The investigators ran the DNA through CODIS, but it hasn't returned any matches yet, but-"

"Okay, just throwin' it out there," Lainey interrupted. "Don't like 60% of the population have one foot that's larger than the other?" she asked hopefully.

"That is correct; they do. I just happen to fall into that 60%," Alessandra offered with a smirk.

Lainey subtly held on to the chair beside her in case there was an earthquake because that woman's porcelain doll face almost never broke into a smile.

"In this case though, X-rays of the feet showed that the bone density is completely different between the two."

She used the remote control to pull up side-by-side overhead images of the two feet that were both sawed off just above the ankle. "As you can see," she said zooming in, "The visible bone of the newer foot has a much lower density. The healthy bone here somewhat resembles a honeycomb. However, in this second image, you can see that the holes and spaces in the honeycomb appear significantly larger than in the first victim's bone. This second man was either over fifty years of age or had a health condition that would cause this... Rheumatoid arthritis, chronic kidney disease, possibly overactive parathyroid gland... Either way, these two feet did not come from the same man."

Before Claudia could even get her question out, Alessandra began to answer it as though she had ESP. "There was very little blood on either of the shoes, so they were both deceased at *least* six hours prior to the feet being removed. And judging by how quickly the skin degraded, I would say that this second foot was frozen after removal. So I'm unable to give you an official time of death."

"Were the techs able to collect any trace evidence from the shoe that you know of?" Claudia asked. "I know they were able to gather some from the first victim's shoe, though it wasn't particularly helpful."

"Yes. I was told they retrieved a soil sample. Much like fingerprints, each soil type possesses unique identification markers," Alessandra explained.

"So if they can locate and identify the soil sample, they can connect the victim to that location," Lainey deduced.

"Exactly. I sent the shoe up to the crime lab, but... Well... There's always some sort of muck, dirt *some*thing in the grooves of the bottom of a worn sneaker. It was almost like the attacker maybe cleaned the shoe before leaving the foot. But they'll be able to tell you more once everything has been processed."

"It was a leather shoe," Lainey commented, walking over to get a closer look at the X-ray. "Hopefully they'll be able to lift some prints?"

"That's possible, but if this attacker took that great of care to remove all the trace particulates *beneath* the shoe, the likelihood that he left fingerprints *on* it is probably slim," Claudia replied. "Thank you for this information."

"You are welcome," she said ever so formally as she placed the tray back into the cooler.

"Okay, how can you possibly have an appetite for lunch after that?" a handsome green-eyed gentleman asked as he strolled into the room toward the M.E. She reached toward him for an embrace, but he backed away quickly. "Your gloves."

"Oh, right, sorry," she said shaking her head, forgetting that she hadn't yet removed the protective gear that recently stood between her and the corpse. "You ladies know my husband, yes?" she asked rhetorically while removing and trashing the black gloves.

"Good afternoon, detectives," he nodded as he flashed them a dazzling smile, observing them through long thick lashes.

Claudia couldn't help but wonder how all of the men get the most striking lashes that women literally have to pay for. "Yes, we're all acquainted. Nice to see you again."

"You as well," he said as the ladies turned to exit the room.

"Ready for lunch?" he asked his wife.

Waiting until they were far enough out of earshot, Lainey was bursting at the seams to get her thoughts out. "Okay you know that I think my Penelope is *every*thing, however... if I were even just a liiiiitle bit straight," she said, snickering.

"Girl, if you don't stop. That man is married."

"Which I am *still* trying to figure out! It keeps me up at night," she joked. "Like what does he *see* in her?"

Claudia snickered, but her smile faded as she took a few seconds to look around and assess her surroundings, searching for anyone familiar.

"Everything okay?" Lainey asked, looking around as well, but unsure of for whom or what.

"Yeah..." Claudia hopped into the car still subtly scanning the block. The lingering feeling that she was being watched ate away at her as they headed back to the station.

5

Claudia gasped in fear causing thick, steamy air to fill her lungs. Gradually turning the lever to stop the blazing water, she quietly slid the shower curtain open and grabbed her towel. Slowly wrapping it around her dripping wet body while listening carefully for the noise that she was positive she just heard, she reached into the cabinet under the sink for her .22 that was concealed, secured to the side. There were various well-hidden guns in every room of her home.

Positioning herself along the wall where the yet-to-be-renovated floorboards creaked the least, she tiptoed down the long narrow hallway. She could hear the faint footsteps and light commotion of the intruder, but her heart raced even louder in her ears. As she snuck down the dimly lit corridor, she peeked around into the guestroom, but all was dark and quiet, so she continued toward the main living area. Claudia couldn't help but wonder if this was another nightmare and if she could just awaken herself, it would all be okay. But she couldn't because it wasn't. Someone was definitely in her house, and it sounded like the noise was coming from the kitchen.

Claudia swung around the corner, her gun aimed, ready to fire. "Holy shit, Hope! You scared the *hell* outta me!" She exhaled in exasperation as she removed her finger from the trigger at the last second, knowing how close she came to shooting her only sibling.

"*Seriously!?*" Hope yelled back breathing heavily from the fright. "I scared *YOU!?*" She sighed loudly, running her hands over her smooth, ebony face, then down her long braided hair.

"My bad. I've just been really on edge lately." Claudia glanced toward the clock, "You're *really* early."

"I know. I'm so sorry, CoCo. Your nephew has been bugging me to death to see that new Marvel movie, so we're going to that tonight. I just wanted to make sure you had this food." Hope continued removing casserole dishes and bowls from canvas bags. "I did call, though. But next time I'm waiting for an answer so you don't accidentally take me out."

Claudia picked up her phone to check on that and any other missed calls. "It's dead," she said apologetically as she put it on the charger.

"I also knocked, but when you didn't answer, I used your hide-a-key. You just live so far away from everything, I didn't wanna have to come back out here and I definitely didn't wanna leave it outside in case some coyote made off with it! You know you're out here living with the wild kingdom."

"You're just so funny tonight, aren't you? Are you a chef or a comedian? I just can't tell these days," she joked, scrunching up her nose.

Definitely the former, because Hope's cuisine was far more amazing than her comedic stylings. Hope had exhibited kitchen creativity as far back as when she was turning a pastry from her Easy-Bake Oven into what could be considered a Michelin Star-rated dish. Claudia, on the other hand, wanted absolutely nothing to do with the kitchen. She had zero interest in doing anything that would dirty dishes, which only created one more chore for her to have to do around the house.

"Thank you so much for making the trip with the meal," she said as she hugged her sister. Even though she was a few inches taller than Hope, being in her warm embrace helped to steady Claudia's racing heart. "And keep the key just in case you ever need it again. I shouldn't have it out there anyway."

"Big facts, *detective*. But all the way out here, the only ones trying to get in are probably a few bears."

"Wow, you're just full of them today! So what did *I* make for dinner tonight?" Claudia asked, fully intending to pass her sister's meal off as her own to impress her dinner guest.

"Well *you,* Chef CoCo, have artfully created a salad with homemade balsamic vinaigrette, parmesan shrimp Florentine with penne whole wheat pasta, homemade garlic knots, and of course, a sweet white wine."

"Wow! And a homemade dulce de leche cheesecake? It sounds like I'm so incredibly talented in the kitchen!" Claudia quipped as she peeked under the foil getting a whiff of the fragrant dessert.

"I know, riiiight!? He'll want to marry you after this meal!" They both laughed. "I'll finish getting this all prepped while you finish getting ready."

"Thanks sis," Claudia said, giving her another embrace.

As she turned toward the bedroom, Hope shouted, "Hey! Don't forget *that*," gesturing to the counter.

"Oh, right." She returned for the gun to take it back to its hiding spot.

From her chest of drawers, Claudia selected one of the many lavender lace bras and matching thong panties, which happened to unintentionally match her pedicure. She wasn't too keen on the manicures, as in her line of work, it never seemed to last that long. So she usually kept her fingernails pretty neutral.

As she applied her scented moisturizer, she stared at her scantily clad body in the full-length mirror. Her therapist suggested that she view her reflection and give herself five verbal affirmations each day in an effort to heal her bodily insecurities. Any other woman would look at her and wonder how she could possibly be insecure with her current physique. Visits five days per week to the department's gym, along with her in-home yoga and meditation sessions, contributed to her athletic 5'8" frame. While her B-cup-sized breasts were smaller than she would prefer, her busty bestie would always laugh telling her that it's just more skin to wash, and more than a mouthful is a waste anyway.

Glancing down at her exposed midsection, she noticed a bruise mysteriously starting to form on her left oblique. It was slightly tender to the touch when she applied the lotion, but she didn't think much about it. What she *did* think about was how it really didn't seem to matter how much cardio or abdominal work she did, Claudia just could not get that lower ab definition that she so desired. As she continued scanning down the length of her hourglass figure, anyone looking would quickly notice that the bottom half of that hourglass held much more sand than the top. Claudia's glutes had glutes. And of course with a thick bottom and thicker thighs comes a little extra cellulite. But in reality, with what she was working with, no man was paying attention to some dimples. They always just wanted a handful.

Claudia found it difficult to deliver those positive affirmations regarding her appearance because all she could see were her flaws, like most people when they look at themselves in the mirror. She chocked it up to human nature and wished she could see herself as everyone else saw her - resembling a slightly younger J. Lo.

Quickly hopping into the fitted light blue dress she selected, Claudia ran her hands down her body to smooth it out and delivered herself just one bodily affirmation. "Your ass looks great right now. You don't need these panties." So she slid them off, stuffed them back into the drawer, and ran into the kitchen while pulling her loose, bra-length, brunette curls up into a tight, slick ponytail.

Claudia peeked out all four living room windows and scanned the area before returning to Hope in the kitchen.

"Here, wear this. It will make you look more chefly."

"Is that even a word?" she asked as she looped the apron over her head and began to tie it behind her back.

Since Hope was quite a bit thicker than Claudia, she had to continue wrapping it around to tie the strings in the front.

"It's a word if I say it is," Hope answered as she grabbed her purse to head out. "The pasta dish is in the oven. It will ding when it's ready. Garlic knots are in the warmer. I set the table for you and the wine is on ice there. Oh, and the salad and dessert are in the fridge. Have fun!"

"You are the best sister ever," she said giving her one last squeeze. "Enjoy the movie and give my little man a hug for me."

Just as Hope opened the door to leave, there stood six feet of silver fox, displaying a full salt and pepper beard that just begged for every woman to run their fingers through it. His deep emerald eyes bore into Hope causing her to momentarily lose her footing. She'd never really had a thing for Caucasian men, but she could do with a few scoops of *this* vanilla.

Claudia broke the awkwardness with an introduction, "Hope, this is Weston. We work together."

"Ohhhh... so you're the one snatching my li'l CoCo into stairwells?" she accused flirtatiously.

"Guilty, but please don't press charges," he smiled with his hands up, one of them holding flowers.

As Weston entered the house, Hope exited clutching her imaginary pearls while mouthing the words "call me" to Claudia.

"CoCo? Hmm, I like it. And you look adorable in that apron. These are for you." His deep robust voice made her melt as he handed her a dozen large lavender roses.

"These are breathtaking, thank you so much!" she gushed while inhaling their fragrant aroma.

"You wear a lot of lavender and other pastels, so I figured I'd go with that," he said, strolling through the entryway and into the main area of the house that boasted an updated open floorplan. "This place is amazing. Far away as hell, but amazing nonetheless. I wish you would have told me to pack a lunch," he said with a chuckle.

"I have an incredible dinner here for you, so you won't need the lunch," she retorted while filling a crystal vase with water.

Standing in front of the enormous sliding glass door beside the fireplace, Weston took note of the amount of land before him. "What made you want to live all the way out here? And is that all your land out there? And who mows all this grass? My goodness! The landscaping looks amazing though."

"Wow, you're just full of questions this evening," Claudia giggled as she wrapped her arms around him from behind, resting the side of her face on his back. She closed her eyes and inhaled his signature fragrance, Burberry Touch. The way it intermingled with his pheromones, he always smelled so edible.

"Sorry, it's just my first time visiting you here. I just wasn't expecting... all this."

"The property belonged to my grandparents on my biological father's side. They owned all four acres when they passed away. Darrell- um, my bio dad, couldn't bear to part with it, but also didn't want to live here. He only had one other daughter who passed away a while ago, so he asked if I wanted to stay here. All I needed to do was upkeep the property and pay the taxes. So I agreed."

Weston turned around, still in her arms. "Well, it looks great... but not as great as you," he smiled and planted his lips softly upon hers. Turning his attention back outside, he asked, "What are you doing with the outside there?"

Claudia glanced around him to see what he was referencing. "Oh yeah, the backhoe. It was just some septic system issues. The many joys of homeownership." Claudia rolled her eyes and slid her fingers teasingly along his arm, leading him over toward the sofa.

"And who are these little guys?" Weston inquired noticing Claudia's oversized aquarium.

"Oh, so this orange one is Tyrion, the black one is Arya, and this feisty blue one is Daenerys."

He looked at her skeptically, "You named your fish after Game of Thrones?"

"Absolutely! It's one of my favorite shows! I'll be forced to question your taste if you disagree."

"That won't be necessary, I concur. But why is this little guy separated from his friends?" he asked, noticing the lone fish in the separate bowl.

"Because *this* little asshole tried to *eat* them! So I changed his name to Joffrey," she smirked.

Weston laughed heartily, "That's very fitting!"

Fortunately, before Weston could bombard Claudia with additional questions, the oven timer went off... but they never made it to the dinner table.

*****

"You were supposed to be here for a nice meal."

"Oh, I ate well," Weston uttered suggestively.

"You did," Claudia giggled. "But you wore a condom, right? You know I don't want babies."

"Seriously? Like, not ever?"

"It takes the patience of a *saint* to parent a toddler." He laughed at her dramatic metaphor.

"No, I'm serious!" Claudia rested her hand on her forehead while gazing to the ceiling as she continued to vent, "That whole need to be so independent except you've been in the world for all of two years, you don't know what the hell you're doing, except you're holding me up! I need to get out of the house. The tantrums because *you* wanna go out wearing Barbie dress up high heels when I just need you to put on these tennis shoes so we can get moving! There, for real, has to be a special place in heaven for anyone who can get through parenting small people with underdeveloped frontal lobes. If I don't negotiate with terrorists at work, I especially refuse to negotiate with one under three feet tall."

Weston removed her hand from her forehead, interlaced his fingers with hers, and gazed into her eyes, "You're so beautiful when you complain about miniature people that you don't even have," he chuckled.

"But all of my friends have them. Hell, *you* have them. Say I'm lying."

"You're not. But what about all the good things? They're so cute. What about when they wrap their little arms around you? It's just pure joy," he said as though he were reminiscing about his own children's toddlerhood.

"I thought that's what I had you for?"

"Except these arms aren't so little," he joked as he draped his large leg over hers to help pull her closer and planted kisses on her neck and shoulder.

"Plus!"

"Oh my gosh, there's more?"

"Yes! You can't even discipline them without getting in trouble. I got tapped on the bum as a child - not often because I was generally well-behaved, and look at me..."

"Yes, look *at* you, a grown-ass woman who still likes to be bent over and spanked," he joked as he stole a kiss and smacked her naked ass cheek under the covers.

"Mmmm there *is* some truth to that, but answer my question."

"Yes, I wore a condom. But it will relieve you to know that I had a vasectomy about seven weeks ago. While I love being a father, our two boys are work. I might as well just erect a WWE ring in my living room. I am done."

"Wow, does your wife know that? Because I feel like at one point she led me to believe that you two were trying for a little girl."

"Yes, she *thinks* we're trying and I haven't gathered the heart or the nerve to tell her the truth just yet."

"I mean, I can kind of see why. She's pretty scary."

"Yeah," he sighed. "Like a beautiful fucking monster."

Claudia stared at Weston secretly wondering if anyone had ever described her that way. She definitely had her moments where she felt like a whole other person.

"I feel like she thinks that adding a child to the family will help improve our marital issues, but that couldn't be further from the case."

"You're such an odd pair. How'd you two even meet?"

Weston began to tell Claudia about their whirlwind courtship that began in Italy. Weston was there on vacation, while she just happened to be visiting home. It was in the airport terminal when he'd heard her before he'd ever even seen her. A heated disagreement ensued between a tall statuesque woman and the gate agent. Whatever she was screaming at him in Italian was laced with anger, but it was the sexiest thing he had ever heard. He was just glad not to be on the receiving end of it. Upon completion of the Italian version of the Riot Act she'd just read that poor guy, Weston watched her stride like she was on a runway in Milan to take a seat in the corner and insert her earbuds.

His heart skipped a few beats when she was seated in the first-class pod across from him on the flight back to the States. When he stood, she exceeded his height by easily six inches, partially due to her high heels. This striking creature was crisp from head to toe in a cream-colored suit and a simple solitaire diamond necklace with matching studs in her ears, all made visible as a result of her short trendy haircut.

Weston couldn't help but wonder who would travel from Italy to America dressed like that. It's such a long flight that it seemed like comfort would take precedence over appearance, as clearly demonstrated by his burgundy Adidas sweatsuit and matching tennis shoes. He was usually a very confident man, but this woman with piercing brown eyes was so stunning, he just couldn't get his wits about him and didn't quite know what to say. But he knew he needed to say *some*thing, so he blurted out the first stupid thing that came into his head. "You are simply stunning. Are you a model?"

Returning his gaze with austerity, she seemed to take offense to that, then introduced herself as *Dr. Alessandra Berardi*. He definitely put his entire size twelve foot in his mouth with that one. In his profession, he knew the first rule of investigation – don't make assumptions.

After profusely apologizing to the stunning woman in white, she softened up just enough for Weston to learn that she was the new medical examiner for Allegheny County and was simply traveling home to visit family before starting the new job. She was equally intrigued to learn that he worked out of the Pittsburgh FBI field office. They spent the entire flight home discussing work, how they got into their respective fields, and crime statistics in the greater Pittsburgh area, which then moved on to interesting places to eat in town. And the rest was history.

Still lying on their sides facing each other with their legs intertwined, Weston nuzzled his nose to hers, "Sooo Claudy, now that I've bored you with my backstory, you hungry? Wanna finally dig into that amazing dinner you slaved over?"

"I have a confession. My sister made that meal. She's a chef," Claudia admitted hiding her head under the sheet in embarrassment.

"I figured as much. There was an "I cook stuff" bumper sticker on the car when I pulled up. But shall we partake anyway?"

"Sure." She ran her finger down his soft hairy chest and took gentle hold of his limp piece. Weston inhaled sharply as it immediately began to stiffen with every stroke of her smooth delicate hand.

"I'd like a taste of *you*," she whispered breathlessly as she flung the covers aside and began to provide expert lip service to his fully engorged manhood - such service he had rarely been acquainted with in his marriage.

6

Claudia entered the office and took her standard seat on the right side of the couch with the thick plush armrest. But feeling antsy, she instead stood up to peruse the large open space. Dr. Sydney Elenna Pearce - that name covered a huge portion of one of the walls on multiple degrees, certificates, and awards she had received over the years. She continued through the room, stopping at the wall of windows.

This beautiful office space with floor-to-ceiling corner windows could not possibly be cheap to rent. Standing in that corner of clear, clean glass made it feel like she wasn't even indoors. Depending where a patient chose to sit, the river was visible through one set of windows and the bustling city street on the other. And anyone who had regular appointments was always privy to what Broadway show was in town, as they were prominently displayed on the Benedum Center's marquee.

Claudia read the "Upcoming Shows" signage which reminded her she needed to grab tickets for Jekyll and Hyde coming next month. She thought about taking Weston and hoped he'd enjoy the variable struggle between good and evil. That's what made it her favorite musical.

From that third-story window, she stood watching pedestrians rush down the streets, but one seemed to be holding up the flow of foot traffic as people rushed and scooted around him in their haste to get to work. The light-skinned gentleman in the navy blue sweatsuit looked up and made eye contact with Claudia. Almost like he knew she was there... With his hands in his pockets, the stranger held eye contact for a few seconds as he slowly strolled down the street. His oddly familiar look sent chills up Claudia's spine even though she couldn't quite place him. Was it from a crime scene? Had he been the one watching her, even though she had no proof that was actually happening?

"Claudia!" Dr. Pearce said as she swiftly entered the room.

Completely focused on the stranger outside, Claudia jumped when she heard her name but turned around smiling, with her hand on her chest.

"So sorry to scare you. And for the delay. I had to take an important phone call."

"That's okay," she replied, taking her original seat.

Dr. Pearce hit record on her mini tape player, grabbed her tablet and pen, and also got comfortable in the chair across from her. "So Claudia. There's something different about you today. You seem to have a... glow about you. Am I wrong in my perception?"

"Well, I've been seeing someone," she blushed.

"Well now! How exciting. What has he done to give you this aura... that smile?"

Claudia bit her lip and looked at Dr. Pearce with a sly smirk.

"Okay. Got it. Nuff said. So is it serious? Or are you just having fun?"

"For now, I'm just having fun. Plot twist, he's a little bit married. I'm probably not supposed to tell you that?"

"This is a safe space; you can tell me anything," Dr. Pearce reminded her. "So, how do you feel about that? Him being married."

"I feel... like... I enjoy his company, but it's still just sex. I could be getting it from him or anyone else. But I *prefer* it from him," she replied with a delicate smile.

"Interesting that you say that because you've recently discussed intimacy with two other people." Dr. Pearce flipped through the pages of her notebook. "Both fellow officers, one a new guy... but you've never displayed this type of visibly positive response toward the others. Perhaps you care more about this fellow than you're willing to let on," she asked as more of a statement than a question.

Claudia pondered her comment but didn't respond. She wasn't sure if it was because Dr. Pearce was correct in her assessment regarding her amorous feelings toward Weston, or if it was because she felt judged. She was positive that wasn't Dr. Pearce's intention but that she was just sensitive about hearing out loud that she had slept with that many men in such a short period of time - not to mention the reminder that she'd slept with the baby-faced rookie, unbeknownst to her nosey partner.

"How did you meet this gentleman?"

"We also work together."

"Oh," she replied in subtle shock. "What are your concerns about any potential conflict regarding these workplace relationships?"

Claudia inhaled deeply, then exhaled slowly. "That's not what I'm *currently* concerned about."

"Go on..."

Claudia stood up and headed away from the doctor back over to the window facing the street. She scanned the concrete jungle for the stranger in blue, but he was no longer there, which was a good thing. "I feel like... like someone's watching me. Like I'm being watched all the time. Miles is still in prison for at least another ten years, so it's definitely not him."

Dr. Pearce remained silent.

"You're staring at me right now. I can literally *feel* your eyes on me." Claudia turned to confirm that Dr. Pearce did, in fact, turn around in her chair and was staring at her, but only in a way that reflected one's good manners to look at the person who's speaking. Eye contact is, after all, how you establish and build a connection with someone.

"How long have you been feeling like this?"

She paused to think about it. "About two months or so... Since that Rossi double murder case when you and I met."

"Ohh yes, I did see on the news that the body part found at the park belonged to him."

"Right. So at least I know *he's* not the one following me. If there even *is* anyone following me. I've never even seen anyone, which is why I didn't want to mention it. I didn't want you to think I was crazy or something," Claudia voiced as she got up again to pace the floor and look out the window. "But I *feel* crazy. Like everyone who makes eye contact with me is suspicious."

"Do you think that it could be because you still feel guilty about the death of the Rossi family and maybe you're manifesting this in your mind?"

Claudia considered her suggestion but didn't believe that to be the case.

"Also, you said that you haven't noticed anyone. But you know, you don't have to *see* someone to be aware of them. Right? It could be that you've come across someone, but they're not important enough to you that you really *notice* them. Does that make sense?"

Claudia considered that as her eyes danced around the room while she reflected on her whereabouts the past few days. After a long sigh when nothing came to mind, "But... what if I was wrong?" she asked contritely. "What if Clem Rossi really *didn't* kill his family? What if the person who killed *them* also dismembered *him*? And that person's just... out there watching... *me*."

"Have you brought this up to your squad?" Dr. Pearce asked with concern, well aware that Claudia has a dangerous occupation. People who feel wronged by her, or her colleagues, for that matter, may very well act upon that ill will. But she chose to keep those thoughts to herself so as to not heighten Claudia's already elevated paranoia.

"Of course I posed that theory, but I didn't mention the rest. All the time though, I'm scanning every face – everywhere I go. I feel like I'm watching for him, whoever *he* is, almost as diligently as he's watching *me*." Claudia paused and sighed in frustration. "I feel like it's impeding my ability to do my best work because this feels personal, and I'm..." She looked away almost ashamed to finish her sentence.

"Scared?" Dr. Pearce asked, unsure if she had the correct emotion and not wanting to put words in her patient's mouth.

Claudia closed her eyes and quietly replied, "Yes," while picking at her nails. "I risk my life daily doing this job, yet that doesn't scare me. *This* does." She paused, looking down at her cuticle that began to bleed. She reached over for a Kleenex before continuing, "I just don't want the captain to think I'm insane and pull me from the case, especially since I haven't actually *seen* anyone. It's just a gut feeling."

"How often is your gut wrong?"

"Almost never."

"That was the crime lab," Lainey said, hanging up the phone at her desk. "They're still working to match soil samples from Clem Rossi's shoe to other samples they have on file from the area. They also said the second shoe was bleached clean and scrubbed down with something. So they found zero trace, other than what was on the incline floor. No fingerprints, no hair, no DNA on the shoe itself, not even the victim's."

Claudia exhaled and rolled her eyes along with rolling her chair back from her desk in frustration. "So if the M.E. believed that the same person committed both dismemberments, that means what? He realized he made a mistake by leaving particulates on the shoe, so he fixed this one up so we wouldn't find anything?"

"So you're thinking it's someone with an extensive knowledge of criminalistics?"

"Well, we won't need to guess much longer," the captain announced, approaching the group of detectives. "The Behavioral Analysis Unit is sending someone over.

He's getting a profile together for us," he continued, popping another piece of gum into his mouth.

They all quietly looked around at each other until a ringing phone broke the silence.

"Be right back," Claudia said quietly to Lainey before making her way to the front desk to address that call.

"Detective Martinez, there's a woman here to see you," Teddy said, nodding in the direction of a slender blonde-haired mother and her mini look-alike daughter.

Before Claudia could make it over to them, they approached her. "Detective. Hi."

"Hello," she replied to the mother and gave the daughter a smile and a wink. "I remember you... Mrs. Holsinger?"

"Brenda, yes, that's me. And my daughter, Gemma. I'm here because of my husband... I think he's missing. I- I found your card in Gemma's room and I didn't know what else to do."

"Okay, well come with me upstairs and we'll get some information from you."

She tapped the front desk and put her hand out to Teddy. He handed her a Dum Dum lollipop that she gave to Gemma, instantly putting a smile on her face, revealing the deepest dimples.

As they waited for the elevator, Claudia recalled visiting the Holsinger home last week for a male/female disturbance call. Though she wouldn't be the person who typically responded to that type of call, she was already in the vicinity. So she answered dispatch back that she would stop by the house. This time, the husband had a documented history of violence toward women, including his wife. So there was little question of whether or not their altercation had turned physical.

Brenda was clearly shaken up but maintained that the disagreement was not physical and was adamant about not pressing charges. She tried to rush Claudia away before her husband could get to the door to see that the police were there, yet again.

When Adam arrived, he aggressively took a place beside his wife and belligerently confirmed the verbal disagreement. He apologized profusely for scaring his daughter enough to call the police.

Throughout their exchange, Claudia could see little Gemma sitting on the steps with her petite fingers wrapped around the white balusters staring back at her with fear and defeat in her enormous gray eyes.

Claudia asked to enter the home, knowing that as long as they granted her access, it was okay. But it seemed like people who enjoyed breaking the law were always so aware of their rights, instead of being more aware of and abiding by the laws they were breaking.

He loudly denied her access to the home without a warrant, said his daughter was fine, and slammed the door shut while continuing to quietly yell at his wife.

Claudia fought the urge to just kick the door in because she refused to have a horrific repeat of the last domestic call. But without sufficient cause, she couldn't legally do it. And because Brenda showed no evidence of injury, she wasn't able to press the charges against him herself.

Through the window beside the door, Claudia could still see Gemma on the stairs. She put her business card up against the window and motioned that she was going to leave it there on the windowsill. She printed on the back of it, "Call me if you need help."

Gemma's nod indicated that she understood. Apparently, she must have gone out to retrieve the card and hid it in what she perceived to be a safe place.

Heading back to her cruiser, Claudia promptly made a call to Children and Youth Services to execute a wellness check. She just hoped that they would be safe through the night.

"So when was the last time you saw your husband, Mrs. Holsinger?" Claudia asked, motioning for her to have a seat beside the desk.

"Brenda, please. And it was the day after you visited," she scowled. "I'm still not happy about you calling C.Y.S."

Claudia exhaled but remained steady. She could not understand why someone in Brenda's situation wouldn't want help getting out of it, if not for herself, at least for the sake of her impressionable daughter. The detective knew firsthand how traumatic it was to grow up thinking it was normal to live in perpetual fear *and* that physical violence was acceptable behavior.

"They came the next day," Brenda continued. "Adam was livid the entire time they spoke with Gemma. She was fine. He would never do anything to hurt her."

"But he hurts *you*. You don't think *that* hurts your daughter?"

Brenda looked away, knowing she was correct, then continued, "He agreed to get help. He even agreed to leave the house in hopes that they would leave Gemma with me and not take her away. They said they'd be back."

"And he hasn't called?"

"No. And his phone just goes straight to voicemail when I call." She paused. "It's just so unlike him – not that I mind. He would call throughout the day, always thinking I'm sneaking around when really I'm taking care of our home and our daughter." With tears forming in her green eyes, she glanced over at six-year-old Gemma, who was showing her stuffy bunny to another detective across the room. "I mean... I couldn't even go to Target alone - for a break! He wouldn't watch his own child. I always had to take her so he knew I wasn't going somewhere to have an affair. I just needed *bread*!" She shrieked before breaking down into tears of exhaustion.

Her scream drew the attention of the room. Claudia wasn't sure how to comfort this woman because part of her was glad that Adam was gone and she didn't particularly care where he was. They would both be better off without him. She knew that was a terrible sentiment and would likely have to work that out in therapy as well. Fortunately, her partner stepped in, offered a tissue, and placed her hand on Brenda's shoulder to help console her. Claudia offered Lainey a look of gratitude.

She continued taking down the necessary information to complete the missing persons report and handed Detective Lockhart Adam's cell phone number to check for the last known location before the phone was turned off.

They all knew that the first 72 hours of a missing persons case were the most critical and that the odds of finding the person alive after that decrease exponentially.

"We will do our best to locate him," Claudia said, doing *her* best to sound empathetic. "In the meantime, you have my card. Call me if you hear anything and we will do the same."

"Thank you... so much."

Detective Burgess escorted Brenda to her daughter and then out of the building.

"That was intense," Lainey commented. "She seemed pretty exasperated."

"Yeah..."

"Little girl's sweet, though."

*****

"Okay, I've finally got something," Lockhart shouted to the room. "Adam's cell phone has not pinged off of any towers since the day his wife said he left. It pinged in a location the next town over and was there for the rest of the day. The last tower it pinged from was the one back in the radius of their home."

"Took you long enough, Rookie," Lainey quipped. "So he went back to the house? Think *she* coulda done something to him?"

"Anything's possible, but I would be shocked," Claudia replied. "If you could have seen her on that call. She was so jittery and fearful of him. I don't believe she would've been able to maintain enough composure for a nice, neat disappearance. If anything, it would be like a desperate act of self-defense or a fit of rage from just being tired of the abuse after all this time."

"Martinez. Crane. Swing by the house today to see if anything is amiss," Higgins barked. "...if anything looks out of sorts. If she has nothing to hide, she'll let you in. If she doesn't, we can see about getting a warrant."

*****

Claudia tried her best to ride to the Holsinger home in silence, but Lainey would have none of that. She chatted non-stop the entire way to the victim's house while Claudia stared out the window, deep in her thoughts.

"...and so I ended up having to send Penelope three dozen red roses! Isn't that crazy? Are you listening to me?"

"Oh, uh yeah... Red roses," Claudia chuckled. "I hate red," she mumbled under her breath as her mind wandered back to her childhood, watching all of her favorite clothes turn red from her mother's blood.

"Are you kidding me? With your beautiful bronze skin, you probably look *amazing* in red."

"Thank you, but I wouldn't know. I never wear it. I carry a gun and a badge all day, I look aggressive enough without wearing the color of... Hey stop! Isn't that Adam's car?"

"That... looks like his tag number."

They pulled up behind the white 2017 Ford Escape that was still running. "We're only three blocks from his house."

Claudia got out of the cruiser with her hand on her firearm, unsure if there was anyone in the vehicle. She looked around then slowly approached to inspect the SUV while Lainey ran the plate that came back registered to Adam Holsinger.

She put on the black disposable gloves, opened the driver's side door, and reached in to turn the car off. Moving to the unlocked back door, she opened it to find a packed duffel. Since it was already unzipped, Claudia peeked in, noticed a pill bottle, then immediately pulled out her phone and opened Google. "Oh shit."

*****

"So, what did you find out?" Captain Higgins came out and asked as soon as he saw his detectives return to the office.

"You want the good news or the bad news first?" Lainey asked.

"Good news."

"Well, we found Adam Holsinger's SUV parked on his street, abandoned but still running, three blocks away from his house."

"To or from?"

"It appeared as though he was on his way back *to* the residence. There was a duffel in the back. Assuming he took that when he left initially. Other than the unlocked car, there was nothing out of sorts. The forensic team impounded it to dust for prints, just in case," Lainey answered.

"Do I even want the bad news?"

"Well," Claudia replied, "That foot likely belongs to Adam. In his bag, I found prescription meds. When I looked it up, it's for joint pain, which would explain the low bone density in that foot, according to the M.E."

Captain Higgins rubbed his temples and shook his head. "Any sort of camera surveillance in the area? Neighborhood cams? Doorbell cams?" he asked.

"So, they live in one of those new housing developments. As soon as you turn onto their street, the first four houses are still being built, so they're vacant. Directly across the street is still a giant empty lot. The house that Adam parked in front of, the owner was kind enough to let us view the footage," Claudia answered.

"The problem is, it's not a Ring doorbell cam. It's an off-brand surveillance cam - one of the much cheaper versions, so the resolution is questionable at best," Lainey interjected while Claudia pulled up the footage on a flash drive.

"Eyes up, everyone!" the captain yelled.

Only the back third of Adam's vehicle was visible on the grainy, low-resolution camera footage. It was clear that his car was running and he was just sitting in it. He then got out of the vehicle and in the darkness, it appeared as though he was talking to someone parked behind him. The driver suddenly turned on the lights intensely illuminating Adam. He shielded his eyes while yelling even more furiously at the driver who was parked far enough behind him that the vehicle was not visible on the camera.

"He walks toward the unknown vehicle out of frame, then that's it. Lights go out. Adam never goes back to his car. His phone cuts off about two minutes after this video footage ends."

"Well, why the hell is there no sound? What the hell's he saying?" Higgins questioned angrily.

"It's just video. There's no audio on this recording system," Lainey replied.

"Get that video over to the FBI's linguistics division - see if they have someone who can read his lips! What about the house?"

"Well, we didn't expect to find anything after we learned that he never made it back there. But she did let us in and didn't seem as though she had anything to hide. She gave us permission to check around the house, basement, garage, and the outside shed."

"And all the land around the house appeared to be undisturbed," Claudia added.

"She gave us his hairbrush, which we dropped off at the lab so they at least have something to compare the DNA to if any more of him turns up."

8

It's a beautiful night to leave the city a gift, I think to myself whilst taking great care to stay on the stony sidewalk versus the quicker route through the damp grass. The last thing I need is more fucking mud involved.

Shrouded in darkness, I am cloaked in black from my ball cap down to the work boots, which are a full size and a half too small. Though exceedingly uncomfortable, there is a method to my particular brand of madness. Should sloppiness inadvertently occur again and footprints ever be lifted, they won't come close to matching my actual shoe size. But I don't plan to ever become a suspect anyway - simply taking the necessary precautions. I continue my stroll through the area staying close to the trees, relatively invisible to passersby, until reaching my intended destination.

While the location is quite visible and there are still many people milling about at the late hour just before closing, no one is paying any attention. It seems like no one ever pays attention. People are either coupled up and involved in themselves, taking selfies, engrossed in social media, or simply sprawled across the concrete staring up at the vast empty sky and enjoying the stars.

Taking a seat to surveil the area once more, I gently lay the black backpack to my left. Well damn. This is almost too easy. Why didn't I bring the rest of the body instead of just this one piece? In such a high-traffic area, one would expect to find cameras, yet there is no video surveillance anywhere. These are some of the stupidest people alive. When I get done, bet you they'll want some cameras then. And better lighting...

Already wearing two pairs of black disposable gloves to avoid transferring even partial prints through them, I slowly, carefully remove the gift from the sterile plastic bag and quietly deposit it into its destination, completely unnoticed. I then remove the gloves, place them inside the plastic bag, and back into my backpack.

To fit in with the self-absorbed people around me, I should behave as they do. I pull out my burner cell phone from my left jacket pocket and fake taking a selfie. Of course it's not turned on. I'm not stupid enough to bring a working phone to a future crime scene.

Satisfied with the performance that I've just given, I throw the backpack over my left shoulder and exit the same way I'd entered.

9

As Claudia's head rested in her hands on her desk, she breathed slowly and deeply trying to mentally prepare for the day ahead.

"You okay?" Detective Tanner Lockhart approached with a cardboard to-go tray holding four coffees and a brown paper bag. "Maybe this will help whatever's bothering you," he said with a warm smile that spread across his baby face.

He removed a large caffeinated beverage and handed it to Claudia, also leaving a steaming cup on Lainey's desk across from hers.

"Oh wow!" Inspecting the iced beverage, Claudia was surprised. "Wait, how did you know what I like to drink?"

"So, it was the weirdest thing. I was just ordering regular small coffees and when the barista noticed my badge and heard your name going on the cup, this is what he gave me instead. Oh, and this. He said you would like the pastry."

Claudia chuckled and shook her head. Levar had written "Enjoy" on the pastry bag with a little heart above the "j" and also added additional hearts after her name on the coffee cup.

"If I didn't know any better, I would say he has a little crush on you. But I mean, who could blame him? Seems like a sweet young guy. I didn't have the heart to tell him about us and that he should fall back."

Claudia closed her eyes, exhaled, and forced a slight rigid smile as she thought to herself, *There is no us. We had sex in the back of your squad car in a dark alley.* After a few more breaths, she finally replied softly, "Hmmm... Well, thank you for this."

Saved by the bell! As her phone rang, she immediately answered it, putting an end to the awkward conversation. That didn't stop her from watching him walk away, because that man had a butt like a male ballet dancer.

*****

The heart of Downtown Pittsburgh was known to beat strongest on beautiful days like today. As happily as the three rivers met at Point State Park, so did the boaters, jet skiers, and kayakers. People hanging out at the water's edge could be seen waving to passengers on the Gateway Clipper gliding down the river. The grassy area behind the stunning fountain that sprays 150 feet into the air was filled with people engaging in activities ranging from yoga classes to reading on a blanket to playing frisbee or catch with the family.

Other visitors, who preferred to be closer to the fountain to feel the mist when the wind blew, took up residence on the nearby steps or on the ledge of the fountain itself. One would be shocked by how many children were fully dressed inside the fountain playing in the water.

Photographers came from everywhere to photograph the heroic monument and every visitor was damn near obligated to take a selfie in front of it.

"To the left," a young visitor said to her friend, snapping pictures to commemorate the experience. "A little bit more... perfect! Now, why don't you try one leaning across the ledge?"

"Are you sure? I don't want to fall in," she replied.

"Stop being so dramatic! That ledge is huge, you'll be fine. And it'll look great on Instagram."

"You're right," she agreed as she climbed up onto the ledge. "Now what should I do?"

"Why are you acting like you've never taken pictures before? Lay down and drape your hair over the side."

She followed her friend's instructions and dramatically positioned her long, loose, reddish waves over the rounded edge of the fountain.

"OMG, this could totally be like a shampoo ad right now - your hair is stunning! Now pose for me, baby," she requested in a fun, flirty manner.

"Wait until you see these! They are so-"

"Nooooo! My stuff!" the girl on the ledge screamed out.

"What happened?" She ran over to her friend.

"My keys and change purse slid out of my pocket into the water."

The friend looked fretful watching her plunge her hand into the questionable fountain water. There was no way to know if it was safe and clean or contaminated river ick.

"I can't reach it. You have to go in for it."

"What!? I'm not digging my arm into that water! Are you crazy?"

"This was *your* idea! Plus, you have on a tank top - your whole arm is available. If I put my arm in any deeper, my entire shirt is gonna get wet. Come on, please?" she begged. "Look, there are like sixteen kids playing in this water – it's fine."

"Ugh... alright!" She acquiesced begrudgingly as she handed over her devices and removed her bracelet. "But you owe me – big time!"

The cold water inside the fountain was less than two feet deep but took up just about all of her arm.

"I think I feel the keys, no wait that's change... Okay, I got 'em!" She pulled the keys out, shook them off, and laid them on the ground beside her feet - not on the ledge where they could accidentally slip in again. She went back in for the miniature change purse but didn't feel it. The force of the fountain may have shifted the item's location. She continued to root around until she had what felt like a familiar object in hand.

"I got it!" she exclaimed, yanking her arm out of the brownish-colored water.

"Holy shit is that a *hand*!?" screamed a young man on a skateboard cruising past. He immediately hopped off at the sight of it.

The girl was still holding it in the air in front of her in shock.

Intrigued, the male passerby quickly came closer to investigate.

"That cannot be real," her friend remarked.

"Oh, that's definitely real! I'm a med student over at Pitt. That's a real hand! You should probably put it down," he said, pulling out his phone to call for help.

Still holding the hand in abject horror, her breathing became irregular, as she was visibly distressed.

The call connected and the young man put it on speaker, "9-1-1, what's your emergency?"

"Hi yeah, I'm at Point State Park and a girl just pulled a human hand out of the fountain."

Her breathing became more uneven on the verge of hyperventilation, still frozen in fear, holding the hand unable to release it.

"Excuse me? What is your name? You *do* know it's illegal to make a false 9-1-1 report, right?"

As she realized what was happening, the decomposing hand slipped out of the girl's grasp onto the ledge of the fountain beside her. A blood-curdling shriek startled everyone in the area as she stared at the slimy cadaver residue on her hand. Mid-scream, she turned to vomit in the water and her friend rushed to hold her hair. Screaming and chaos erupted around the fountain when people began to realize what was happening. Parents hastily snatched their children from the water, where they shouldn't have been playing in the first place.

"Now do you believe me?" the man sarcastically said to the 9-1-1 operator.

"Oh wow, um, park rangers and employees are on the premises already; I will send them over. Please stay on the line with me until they arrive."

"*Park Rangers* in the middle of *Pittsburgh*? That's a thing? Don't we need *real* cops for this?"

"They *are* real officers and they should be to you momentarily."

The young man disconnected the call as soon as he saw a tall uniformed guard who looked to be in his mid-sixties. He pushed against the flow of the crowd that was frantically rushing toward the park's exit.

Upon surveying the gruesome scene, the gray-bearded man threw both hands into the air and shook his head. "Is that what I *think* it is?" he asked, backing away from the putrefying limb. "Awwww, HELL naw! Not today! I was supposed to have retired three years ago! I *quit*!!" he yelled, throwing his hat to the ground and then kicking it. "They don't *pay* me enough to deal with this shit! Call somebody else! Y'all crazy as hell!" The park employee continued grumbling, which trailed off as he walked away from the scene, still shaking his head, "All them bodies they just found in the river and now the *dead* hand!? Nope... Uh-uh, *nope...*"

The three youngsters stood staring at each other in wide-eyed disbelief, as the girl consoled her hyperventilating friend.

"9-1-1, what's your emergency?"

"Yeah, me again. So the guy the first operator sent over here to The Point? He just quit."

*****

Claudia and Lainey arrived on the scene to find the M.E. and Pittsburgh Police talking to the federal rangers in charge of patrolling city parks.

"Officer, this is not your jurisdiction," Ranger Suarez could be overheard reminding the local officer.

"Maybe not," Claudia interjected, approaching them with an authoritative tone, "but that dismembered limb over there clearly falls within a case that the Violent Crimes Unit is working on with the FBI to apprehend a serial killer. So, if you wouldn't mind stepping aside and letting my people through. Otherwise, I'm glad to make a quick call to inform the mayor who held up our investigation."

Ranger Suarez scowled at the detectives, but he reluctantly stepped aside and extended his arm, indicating they could proceed. "Just... keep us in the loop, please."

Lainey nodded in agreement as they continued toward the crime scene.

Claudia loudly exhaled and carefully observed the entire scene. New arrivals to the park were met with bright yellow wooden DO NOT ENTER barriers across the edge of the grass that prohibited them from getting any closer to the giant water feature. It had been turned off but it really didn't matter. By then, with the constant motion, siphoning, and force of water, any additional trace evidence would have long been displaced.

She continued to methodically analyze everyone's faces for anyone who looked even vaguely familiar. *I know you're here at my crime scene. Which one are you?*

"Laura." Claudia motioned for the CSI to come closer, "I want pictures of every one of these people. Be discreet about it but photograph everything and everyone. I want to compare these images to the previous crime scene photos. Is there anyone repeatedly showing up in all these photos?"

"You!" She motioned to one of the newer investigators whose name she hadn't yet committed to memory. "I want this garbage. All of it in the park - every trash can. That hand had to have been transported here in something. If we're lucky, the perp tossed it on the way out."

"If this *is* the same perp, he has graduated from feet to hands. He bleached the last shoe, so I don't know that you'll *be* that lucky," Dr. Berardi remarked curtly before nodding and exiting the scene with the limb.

10

Claudia & Lainey arrived at the medical examiner's office only to find Alessandra with her husband, Weston.

They slowly entered the room, "Good morning, sorry, hope we're not interrupting." Even though, secretly Claudia was glad to intrude on their time together. She knew her therapist was right about her feelings regarding Weston, even though she wasn't ready to admit them. He'd told her he was ending the marriage, but it wasn't happening quickly enough in Claudia's opinion.

"It's no bother," Alessandra replied tersely, "Weston was just leaving anyway."

"Yeah... uh... just here to pick up some additional information on that hand. I have a few other stops to make, then I'm headed over to your precinct to discuss the profile of your unsub."

"Perfect." Claudia awkwardly smiled, trying to avoid eye contact with him. Alessandra took a deep breath in through her nose, out through her mouth, and keenly observed the interaction between her husband and the detectives. Claudia could feel the scrutiny in addition to the tension in the air, and she couldn't help but wonder, does his wife know?

As Weston gathered his files, Alessandra approached him, closed her eyes, and delivered a seemingly passionate kiss goodbye. It was clearly unexpected on Weston's end, as he returned the kiss with open eyes glancing over to the detectives briefly in the middle of it. He gently grabbed her arms and moved her back to end the kiss. Smiling uncomfortably, he looked around at all the women with his mouth now the color of blood from her *fire and fellatio red* lipstick.

"Okay... Yeah... Uh... So..." still awkwardly collecting his items, Weston pointed to the detectives, "I'll see you ladies later," then pointed to his wife, "and I'll see you tonight."

He departed the room with his head down, but not before grabbing a Kleenex from the box to remove Alessandra's unexpected affection from his lips. It simply reminded him that was just one of the many things he admired about Claudia – she wore a fresh, natural face.

Alessandra focused her attention back on the detectives, "So, I don't have as much as I had hoped. This hand was sawed off just above the wrist, same as the feet we found." She pulled up an image on the flat-screen monitor. "The same instrumentation was likely used. Techs have been testing different methods of cutting to see if they can determine which tool would leave cut patterns that match the three limbs. As for the hand itself, much like the previous body parts, the owner was deceased for at least six hours prior to removal. However, because it had been frozen, thawed, already begun to decompose, and then was left submerged in partially moving water for a length of time, severe skin sloughing has occurred. There was a large amount of debris and particulates collected, but I question if they'll be able to differentiate whether or not it came from your assailant, or the water in the fountain - unless it happens to match debris collected from previous victims."

"So that means you weren't able to lift fingerprints to identify this victim?"

"I was not. We will have to rely on DNA for this ID and hope that he's in the system... or that you locate the remainder of the body to match it to."

*****

"It's all hands on deck. I want everyone on high alert, eyes open," Captain Higgins announced to a room full of officers and detectives seated auditorium-style in the large briefing room. "Most of you are already familiar with Agent Weston Grant. But for those who aren't, he's one of the criminal behavioral analysts with the Behavioral Analysis Unit Downtown. He's here to help us figure out who we should be looking for."

"It's good to see you all today, though I wish it were under better circumstances."

As he began to confidently deliver the profile of their perp, all ears and eyes focused on Weston, especially Claudia's. But her mind began to wander. Hearing his deep whiskey-smooth voice, her thoughts drifted to the last time they were together. He stood behind Claudia, his strong arms enveloping her as he swayed them to and fro, whispering how much he craved her.

"The Unknown Subject is presumably a single, 30-to-40-year-old, white male who likely lives in seclusion. He seeks out this isolation because it's possible he was raised in an abusive home and is perhaps still seeking a safe haven."

As he continued speaking with his hands, her mind drifted to him using them to forcefully pin hers above her head against the glass sliding door as he passionately took her mouth with his.

"Murders, where mutilation and dismemberment are involved, are highly associated with childhood sexual victimization. A person who has suffered that type of childhood trauma often suppresses that pain and rage. Former victims might later in life commit crimes to release those suppressed feelings," Weston explained, pacing the front of the room.

Claudia watched his perfectly-shaped lips move while thinking about him using them to plant kisses down her midsection and below.

"It's possible that he may have witnessed similar acts growing up – such as being raised on a farm or by a butcher, where cutting through body parts was considered normal and acceptable behavior."

She subtly licked her lips as her eyes wandered down his midsection and all she could think of was him deeply and adeptly driving his body into hers.

Noticing that Claudia seemed to be elsewhere in thought, Lainey nudged her with her pointy elbow just as Weston began to make his final comments.

"So far, both victims came from homes where your officers and/or detectives paid visits for domestic violence. Each home had a spouse and a child who either *were* or would possibly *be* put at risk. I would wager that your unsub also grew up an only child. His objective is to punish the abuser before additional harm can come to the child." He paused. "Also, he has likely made an appearance at many, if not all, of your crime scenes to revel in his handiwork."

"Where are we at on cross-referencing all of the crime scene photos?" Captain Higgins asked the group.

"We just received the printed images for the most recent incident, but no one stood out at first glance. We'll deep dive further today," Claudia answered.

"Good. Go through them again… And again. I want multiple eyes on this. I can't keep having body parts show up all over town!"

The room remained still, waiting to see if there was more to come, "THAT MEANS NOW! GO!" Higgins roared, which prompted everyone to finally get up and rush out of the room.

Lainey grabbed the thick stack of photos from her desk and followed Claudia and three other detectives into another conference room. They separated the three files and spread the images out on the giant conference table to get a fuller view of each crime scene's spectators. Weston noticed them all through the partially frosted glass wall that separated that conference room from the rest of the squad room. "Mind if I join in?"

"Not at all," Burgess replied. "The more eyes, the better. These are the images of everyone behind the barriers in the first crime scene here, the second, and then the third there," he said, pointing to the respective sets of pictures.

They all silently drifted among the piles of images looking for anyone familiar or similar at all three locations.

Captain Higgins entered the room and gruffly announced, "The mayor's so far up my ass, my doctor gave him a scope for the colonoscopy. So? Tell me you found something."

"At the first scene in Schenley Park, back when we thought this was just a one-off, the spectators weren't the focal point. We only have them in the background of the photos Laura took. At the second scene, at the top of the incline, same thing, there are a few photos of spectators in the background. However, the third scene at Point State Park, pictures were taken specifically of the spectators."

"As you can see," Claudia interjected, "at the first scene, we have this man wearing black sunglasses and a blue jacket. Then at the third scene, you could almost miss it, but the same blue jacket is walking away."

"As though he noticed the camera being pointed in the public's direction, so he needed to get outta there?"

Claudia felt a knot grow in the pit of her stomach. Could that have been the same person she saw at her therapy appointment the other day? Was she the real connection and the reason these men had been murdered? Was someone stalking her cases?

"Were the rangers able to send over camera footage that grabs him at a different angle exiting the park?" Captain Higgins asked.

The room fell quiet as looks were exchanged among the group until a brave soul spoke up, "Sir... there are no cameras... at Point State Park," he said meekly, knowing that the captain may very well blow his top.

"No," he said, shaking his head adamantly. "That's not true. They installed them last year. It was approved after they found all of those cars and bodies piled up in the river."

"It may have been approved, but the project was never executed. Red tape. Funding... Yada yada."

Higgins patted his pants in search of his pack of gum, "What about the second crime scene at the incline? No sign of Blue Jacket?"

"The incline docked at the top, so that's where we all ended up. But there would be no way of knowing when the foot would be discovered - on the way up or down. Possibly our perp took a 50/50 shot and guessed wrong? He could've been at the bottom where everything was roped off, but we have no images of spectators there."

"And of course, no camera footage because the cameras were out."

"Yes sir."

"What about facial rec?" the rookie detective asked.

"Unfortunately, since he was in the process of turning away from the camera and wearing sunglasses, there's not enough of his face available for the facial recognition software to be effective. Plus, since he's not the focal point of the image, he's just a blur in the background."

Captain Higgins rubbed his hand down his entire face in exasperation. He stared at the pack of Nicorette gum for a few seconds, then threw it in the trash on the way out of the conference room. "I'm gonna get a cigarette," he resigned.

11

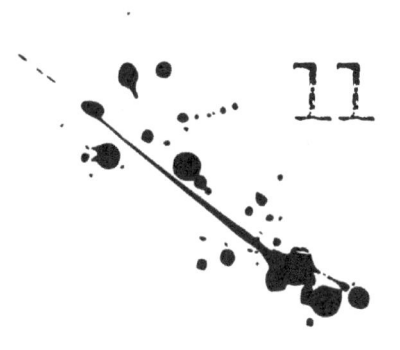

"We're all goin' out for drinks tonight after shift," Lainey announced to Claudia.

"Sorry babe, but I already have plans for this evening."

"With *who*!? I mean... Sorry, we just really need to go out and have a drink... *tonight*."

"What's so important about tonight that can't wait until tomorrow? The bar isn't going anywhere."

Lainey walked over to Claudia's desk and leaned in, "So I'm not supposed to tell you this, but a few people decided to meet up to celebrate your birthday. You never have plans and we often grab a drink after work, so your sister didn't think it would be that difficult to get you to the bar right quick."

"My sister? Hope?"

"Yeah. It was supposed to be a surprise, so if you could just act like we never had this conversation and that you came of your own volition, that'd be great."

"But my birthday isn't until next week."

"And this is why it's called a surprise, love." Lainey winked and returned to her desk.

Claudia had never cared much for celebrating her birthday considering her mother was killed the day before her Little Mermaid pool party, which obviously never took place. She spent the first day of her seventh year scared and alone in a children's group home until the Jacobs took her in a few weeks later. It's all her fault, though, because she never expressed to her family or friends how painful this time of the year was for her. She just accepted their plans and let everyone do what they wanted.

Claudia realized there was zero point in arguing with Lainey, and she didn't want to disappoint Hope, so she resigned herself to the plan. She just needed to make a quick call first.

Outside the station, a one-sided conversation could be overheard, "Hey... So I'm not gonna be able to see you tonight... My birthday is coming up and Hope invited all these people to celebrate... Wellll, *that's* because they don't know about us, so of course Lainey wouldn't think to invite you... Exactly, especially if you'd be bringing your *friendly* neighborhood medical examiner," Claudia laughed. "I know, I'm sorry. I really wanted to see you too... Southern Tier Brewery... Probably around 7:00 if the city can act right and stop breaking the damn law..."

Claudia didn't say anything else. She just stood leaning against one of the police cruisers listening to whatever it was Weston was saying that put a goofy grin on her face, then hung up the phone.

Completely immersed in her naughty thoughts and conversation, she didn't even notice listening ears were in the vicinity. "I'm sorry, I- I wasn't eavesdropping or anything. I just was walking by. On my way to work," Levar pointed in the direction of the coffee shop. "So, your birthday, huh?"

"Yeah," Claudia shrugged. "It's just another day to me, though."

"Well, you know I'll hook you up with a special birthday treat, on me," he smiled.

"You're too kind, thank you," she said as she made her way back into the building. "Have a good day."

"You too," he replied, watching her until she was no longer in sight.

*****

Weston sat at the head of the dinner table staring down at his plate, not eating but simply moving the food around with his fork. He thought about how a mere eight months after meeting on that flight home from Italy, he and Alessandra were wed in an intimate outdoor ceremony overlooking the water. There were a few skeptical family members who thought she was only marrying him for a green card, but once they'd learned that she was actually already a U.S. citizen, they seemed much more supportive of the relationship. Not that it was any of their business anyway.

Seven years and a set of twin boys later, Weston was miserable in his marriage, and he had assured Claudia that he only stayed so his sons didn't have to know what it was like to be raised without their father around daily, as *he* had known all too well. Even though Weston was unhappy, he continued to treat Alessandra well and show her love in front of their sons. He felt that to know how to treat a woman, seeing it in action while growing up was truly the best lesson - one Weston never received, as his father continually verbally and emotionally abused his mother before walking out on them. He was determined to be a better father, though having an affair with the detective was certainly not the best example to set.

He watched his six-year-old twin boys, seated across from one another, laugh and make jokes between bites, then observed his stunning wife at the other end of the table. She was so beautiful with cheekbones that could've been sculpted by Michelangelo himself. Then his thoughts shifted back to Claudia and the fun they must be having right now celebrating. As much as he loved his family, he never had that type of fun with Alessandra – maybe with the boys, but definitely not with his wife.

He was always so entranced by her appearance and how she carried herself, he clearly hadn't considered the other important components that would bring joy to a relationship – a sense of humor, open-mindedness, a desire to explore, ease of communication. All attributes that Claudia brought to the table, in addition to her physical features that Weston appreciated so much.

Instead, to this table Alessandra brought money, status, and clout. It was only after they had wed that he learned of her financial prominence. She came from one of the wealthiest families in Italy but chose this career path because it was what she loved and wanted to do with her life. She didn't *need* to work, she simply wanted to. Thus the seven-bed, six-bath, state-of-the-art home in the

Heights of Sewickley was purchased by his wife. He didn't need a home with a four-car garage because, in his mind, two people didn't need four cars. Alessandra insisted upon a home with a full-sized, in-ground pool out back, but he would have been fine taking his kids to the community pool to make friends with local neighborhood children like he did growing up.

The luxury vehicles, high-end clothing, designer purses and shoes, she handled all of that. Weston never felt like there was anything he could do for or give his wife, other than their two boys. He felt less like a real provider and more like a glorified security guard to protect the house and a service stud for her own sexual gratification. She took *that* whenever she wanted, but wouldn't even take his last name. Weston understood with her level of education, academic success, and medical publications, of course she would want to maintain her identity, so he merely suggested adding his on and hyphenating. She had agreed but never actually followed through with it. So he didn't press the issue any further. He did, however, draw the line when it came to hyphenating his sons' last names as Berardi-Grant. He'd won that battle, but probably only because after a rough birth, she was in and out of consciousness, so he handled the birth certificate situation.

To anyone looking in, it would appear to be a beautifully perfect life. But Weston just felt trapped. He thought about Claudia and how much she made him laugh, and how she appreciated the little things. Weston couldn't even give Alessandra flowers. She had no interest unless they were sparkling black roses imported from Holland or something equally as insane and expensive.

"Weston dear, you're not eating. What's wrong?" she questioned with not much actual concern in her tone.

Pulled away from his thoughts, "Oh... Uh, nothing. I'm just not too hungry right now. Sorry."

"Dad, we're done eating. Can we be excused to go play?"

He smiled warmly and tousled his son's dark brown hair, "You sure can, buddy-"

"Is that how we ask?" Alessandra interrupted.

"Sorry Mum, mayyyy we be excused?"

"Better. And you may," she replied with little warmth.

Weston rolled his eyes and delivered a lengthy exhale. "Really, Alessandra?"

"*I'm* raising proper young gentlemen here. What are *you* doing?"

"I think... what I'm doing is leaving." He collected his and the boys' plates and silverware. "I need some fresh air."

"Wait. I'm sorry, please sit for a minute. We really need to talk."

"Fine." Weston took the plates to the sink, rinsed and placed them in the dishwasher, then reclaimed his seat at her table. "So... what do you need to discuss," he spewed as a statement, not a question.

"Well, I was going to wait to tell you, but... we are... having another baby. I'm pregnant!" she announced with a serene smile.

Several seconds passed before he was able to respond, as he thought about that timeline. His vasectomy took place well before a pregnancy could've occurred. In a low voice he rumbled, "You absolutely are *not* pregnant, Alessandra."

She went over to her black Christian Louboutin tote and brought an item over to Weston. Draping her arm around his shoulder and taking a seat on his lap, she set the positive pregnancy test in front of him on the table.

Weston heard and felt his heart pumping like it was going to beat right out of his burly chest. He looked at the bright pink plus sign on the test then glared up at her, still seated on his left leg. He did everything in his power to drive his anger back down, but the only thought that ran through his throbbing head was to reach up, wrap his hands around her perfectly slender neck, and *squeeze* until the life slowly drained from her body.

Instead, Weston steadied his breathing, gently removed Alessandra's arm from around his shoulder, and lifted her from his lap. He gave her the tightest peck on the cheek and walked out of the house before he succumbed to the rage coursing through his veins. He sat in his car for a few minutes to calm down, then realized that he needed to see Claudia.

Alessandra stood at the giant bay window perplexed and mildly disappointed as she watched her husband's black Tesla pull out of their driveway. She immediately located her phone and pulled up the Tesla mobile app to not only track his current trip but also to see just where all Weston had been.

*****

The front glass wall of the bar was open so that patrons could spill outside on beautiful warm nights. Lainey was friends with the owner, who reserved her the large set of tables adjacent to the bar.

Even though Claudia had no interest in celebrating, she was having a great time with everyone. She was even more excited to be out with Hope because her sister rarely spent extended time away from the house without the children. Even a few of the officers, who were on duty and still in uniform, stopped by briefly for hugs, birthday wishes, and cake to go.

Though she still couldn't shake the feeling that she was being watched, she was surrounded by law enforcement and never felt safer. That still didn't stop her from periodically scanning the room for suspicious faces.

"Luke! We need another round of shots!" Hope shouted to the bartender.

"No, we really don't."

"Oh yeah! It's your birthday! We're doin' this shit up right!"

Before Claudia could further object, a third round of shots was being distributed to the group.

Tanner leaned into Claudia and whispered in her ear, "If you like, I could take this as a body shot." She laughed, put her hand on his chest, and pushed him away, then they both took a shot, still laughing.

Just as Weston was about to pull open the large glass door to enter the bar, he caught a glimpse of Claudia. He watched Detective Tanner Lockhart whisper in her ear while she smiled with her hand on his chest. His jealousy subsided *some* when she pushed him away and continued drinking and socializing with her friends, but it still infuriated him that another man was so close to her. But it was her celebration and she looked so happy that it would be selfish for him to unload his issues on her right then. He felt like she would be pleased to see him if he were there, but technically he wasn't invited, so Weston retreated to his car parked across the street and watched them for the next few hours, participating in the celebration from afar.

A waitress approached and set a drink down in front of Claudia, "A birthday drink... from an admirer," she said loudly over the music.

"From who?" Claudia asked nervously.

"Not sure," the waitress replied, clearly too busy to engage in conversation.

"Do you know what he looked like?"

But the waitress was already walking away to deliver the remaining drinks on her tray to another table. Claudia stared down at the glass and apprehensively picked it up.

"Oh, you already have one," Tanner observed on his way back from the bar holding two drinks.

Claudia set the gifted drink down in the middle of the table, "No, this was sent to me," she replied, looking around the room. "But I don't know from who."

"Yeah, you don't wanna drink that then. Here. Try this." He smiled, handing her a beverage that smelled of peaches.

"Thanks." They clinked glasses and both took a sip. "Oh wow, that's *soooo* good!"

By the end of the evening, while Claudia wasn't the drunkest she had ever been in her life, she was in no condition to drive back home. Really, she just felt more woozy than actual drunkenness.

"I'm calling her an Uber," Lainey said.

"I can drop her off at home," Tanner offered. "Besides, do you know how much an Uber will cost to get to her place?"

"How do *you* know where she lives, rookie?" Lainey asked suspiciously.

"I mean... I don't know *exactly* where, but remember when she told us the story about the coyotes? I just know it's not close."

"Mmm hmmm..." Lainey replied skeptically. "Are you even fit to drive?"

"Yes ma'am, I'm on duty tomorrow, so I had mostly water."

"Fine."

Still staked out in his car across the street, Weston watched as Tanner escorted an impaired Claudia to her vehicle. She was barely walking on her own as Tanner helped support her weight.

By the time they had made it to Claudia's house, she was so incredibly dizzy.

"Here, lemme help you in," Tanner insisted.

"No, I'm okay. I got it," Claudia murmured as she fumbled with the keys, clearly unable to connect with the lock.

He put his large hand over hers and guided the key smoothly into the hole, staring down at her as they turned the lock to open the door.

"Thanks," she said, stumbling into the house.

Tanner tapped the door shut with his foot and held a very unsteady Claudia close to him. He gazed into her glassy hazel eyes and stroked her cheek with his thumb. Staring at her full glistening lips, he softly kissed her. She exhaled and kissed him back, but then stopped. "No, I- we can't do this."

Still holding her in his arms, he whispered, "You know you want to, Claudia... It's not like we haven't done it before," and continued his sexual pursuit.

"I- I feel... like..." And just like that, her body fell limp in his arms as everything went fuzzy, then faded to black.

*****

Seated on the bed beside her, she could smell the stench of alcohol and cigarettes emanating from his person. He used his middle finger to slide her curls from her exquisite face, then slowly ran that finger down her jawline and across her lower lip. As badly as she wanted to, there was nothing she could do to stop him. The tracing continued down her chin, to her neck where it lingered... then slid down the center of her body to her sweet spot. Her heart raced and her breathing became erratic as he climbed into the bed beside her. She wanted to reach for her gun, but she couldn't move. She tried to scream but nothing came out. *Scream, damn it! CLAUDIA, SCREAM!*

She finally did as she jolted herself upright in another cold sweat, barely able to catch her breath from the other night terror that had been plaguing her the past few years. Much like in the other dream, she was unable to defend herself or see the person who seemed to take great joy in terrifying her. She began to take deep breaths to lower her heart rate, which was off of the charts according to her Apple watch.

Assessing her surroundings, she realized she wasn't even in her bed. She sat running her hands over her body in the darkness wondering how she ended up on the couch and in a cami and panties, no less. Pulling at her hair, Claudia was willing the memories to return from last night, but they were slow to restore.

"Shit!" She hissed as her toe met the end table on her way to the kitchen.

Claudia stood at the island facing the living room. She sipped her water in the dark, listening to the trickle of her aquarium. It was a peaceful sound that always helped calm her.

She slowly made her way over to it, unable to remember if she had even fed the fish. Approaching the tank, Claudia jumped when her bare feet stepped into a cool puddle. She quickly flipped on the tank's blue night light and lost her breath again. She backed up shaking her head in disbelief until she reached the wall to flip on the overhead light. Joffrey's fish bowl had been knocked over onto the floor and he had been placed into the main aquarium. Joffrey swam happily around the open space fully sated after consuming the other three smaller fish.

Floating remnants were all that remained of Tyrion, Daenerys, and Arya.

12

Someone has a birthday coming up. How fun it's been celebrating with her... She will likely don some tight, hideous, pastel-colored frock. But she's such a whore, it never stays on too long.

Stepping into the shop, I can smell the sugar permeating the air so strongly that I can almost taste it. Such an array of tasty colorful options from which to choose... Cherries Jubilee? Strawberries and Cream, perhaps? Maybe the Red Velvet? Red sweets would surely mess with her mind. But I want her to actually crave and desire it. As my eyes dance across the case, there it sits. The last one... all alone like it is meant especially for this occasion. It beckons me like a shimmering pot of gold at the other end of my own little perverse rainbow. A Lemon Lavender cupcake. Moist, citrus-flavored cake topped with almost three inches of thick, creamy lavender flavored and colored icing. The tiny lemon shavings along with the sprig of lavender accent the dessert exceptionally well. She will adore this.

"May I please have this one? And a red velvet for myself. Box them separately."

13

Claudia sat in tears in Dr. Pearce's office thanking her profusely for moving up her appointment. She was unable to get her emotions under control as she relayed the events of the previous evening. While a pet owner could only be so attached to a few fish, it was less about them and more about the fact that someone had invaded her safe space. Her home.

Usually, the doctor was phenomenal when it came to maintaining a neutral appearance, but she could not visibly hide her pain and empathy at that moment for her patient. "What leads you to believe that Tanner wasn't somehow involved, considering he was the last person to see you?"

"It couldn't have been him. I- I thought it was. I knew it was. I accused him! Yelled at him on his way to work! I know people had to have overheard me," she said remorsefully with a hand on her head. "But now, I don't think it was."

"How can you be so sure?"

"I didn't remember getting home - only up to the point where someone sent me a drink last night."

"Did you drink it?"

"I couldn't remember. So I called Lainey, hoping she could fill in some gaps. She said that I didn't have the drink but recalled Tanner bringing me one, and then at the end of the night, he insisted upon taking me home."

"Then what happened?" Dr. Pearce asked softly.

"So naturally, I FaceTimed Tanner. I was *livid*! I accused him of drugging me and murdering my fish!"

"How did he respond to that?"

"Well, of course he denied it and was insulted that I would make such accusations... He texted me over a $58 Uber receipt," she said, shaking her head as she walked over to the glass wall to stare out at the water. "Apparently, he didn't take me home in his car. He drove *mine*, which meant he needed to get back into town to get his. He told me that he thought we were gonna have sex, but then I passed out in his arms. So he carried me over to the couch, removed my shoes and pants for comfort, and the shirt in case I threw up. Then covered me with a blanket and put the trash can next to the couch just in case. Says he waited for the Uber and left."

"And you believe him?" Dr. Pearce questioned.

"After I thought about it... I *guess*? When I woke up from that horrible nightmare," she said, walking back to her seat, "I remember kicking the blanket off. My panties were still on - the same ones I had on. I mean, no man would put the underwear *back on* an unconscious woman after sex, right? Plus, I just didn't *feel*... like... I'd had sex. Ya know? And, then his Uber receipt..."

"I understand. Did you go to the hospital anyway?"

"I didn't," she replied, walking back over to the window and scanning the pedestrians in motion for anyone who looked familiar. "I went to a friend in the lab for a blood draw and requested a tox screen - anonymously, of course. She's gonna put a rush on it to see if I was drugged or not."

"Claudia, the fact that you were able to wake up and immediately recall your dream so clearly, would lead me to believe that you were not drugged."

"Then why can't I remember anything else?"

Silence befell the room.

"Can you tell me more about the nightmare?"

Claudia scanned the crowd once more before walking back over and taking her seat. "I don't know. It's the same as the other one," she said, tapping her foot. "Always the same two dreams over and over. As strong and capable as I am, I'm unable to move or defend myself in either of those dreams and it is so incredibly... *frustrating*!" She began to tear up, "He's in my *home*, he's touching my *body* and there's nothing I can do to stop it. And the most disturbing part of it all is that I find myself becoming physically aroused even though I don't *want* it," she broke down again. "I don't know what to do. I feel so... *guilty*."

"This may not be as helpful as you'd like, but that response is not uncommon. It's merely physiological. Bodies respond to sexual stimulation, period. I'm not going to tell you not to feel that guilt because I understand that it's much easier said than done. But it's something we can work on if you'd like."

Dr. Pearce had some theories. She wasn't sure if Claudia was equipped to tackle them, but she decided to gingerly broach the topic anyway. After handing her a Kleenex, she softly asked, "I know you didn't have a relationship with your biological father, and Miles went to prison. How was your relationship with your adoptive father growing up? We don't talk about him much."

"Umm, really good," Claudia replied, a bit confused. "He was really supportive, always around throughout my childhood, even as an adult... until his work accident," she shook her head, unable to think of anything else to say at that moment.

"Okay, good. So he was never abusive in any way toward you and your sister... physically... verbally..." Dr. Pearce paused. "Any other way?"

"Absolutely not," Claudia replied adamantly. "If you ask me, of all three fathers I've had, the wrong one died. I would gladly trade the other two if it would bring him back," she said sadly.

Dr. Pearce nodded while continuing to take notes. "What do you think about taking a few weeks off to relax and reclaim some of your peace? How's that sound?"

Before Claudia could object, Dr. Pearce amended her suggestion, "Or at least a few days?"

Still tapping her foot and picking at her thumbnail, Claudia hesitantly nodded in agreement.

*****

For once, she heeded Dr. Pearce's work-related advice and took the next two days off. She was also correct about the fact that the tox screen came back negative. No drugs were found in Claudia's system, which was even more bizarre to her.

As her memory slowly returned, the events of that evening kept replaying in Claudia's mind. *Who sent that drink? How could someone have gotten into my home when there was no sign of forced entry? The hide-a-key is empty – gave it to my sister. She's not driving out here just to kill my fish. Who, other than Tanner, who was already here, would want to travel out here? I'm asking the wrong questions. A better one is who all knew the story of why those fish couldn't intermingle?* The issue was that the only ones who knew were all so close to Claudia that she couldn't envision any of them sneaking into her home and doing such a thing.

She checked the entire exterior perimeter of the property for any way in and looked for any footprints since it had rained recently. But everything was locked and secure... until she made it to the basement door. It was an older wooden door that clearly should've been moved up on the renovation priority list. It looked like it could've been tampered with, but it was so old, Claudia couldn't tell if it actually was manipulated or if it had always looked like that and she'd just never noticed before.

That weekend, Weston was kind enough to come over and help her secure that entrance until the arrival of the security door she'd ordered to replace it.

Claudia also added a new home security system with outdoor cameras to the house, something she'd never thought to do because living so far away from civilization, she had always felt safe before these recent cases. Now her safety felt like a distant memory.

Claudia gently set two ice-cold cans of ginger ale on the patio table as she joined Weston seated outside on the deck.

"I appreciate your help today," Claudia expressed.

"Any time," Weston replied, opening his Canada Dry. As Claudia stared into the dense woods ahead, Weston studied her face. He had so many questions, but he didn't want her to know he was at the bar that night or bring up any fearful memories. He figured whenever she was ready to talk to him about it, she would.

They sat out on her deck for hours chatting, drinking, and snacking until the setting sun turned the sky a fiery burnt orange and the stridulation of the locusts filled the otherwise silent space.

"So... Alessandra is pregnant."

Claudia almost spit her drink out. "With *what*!?"

"Exactly," Weston said, shaking his head. "I have an appointment with my urologist in two weeks to see if there's any chance that they botched the procedure and there are still any swimmers. Otherwise..."

"She's been having an affair as well," Claudia interjected.

"Yes. And I know I shouldn't have been angry because I'm no better, but I was infuriated. Horrible thoughts... I just had all of them at once and knew I had to leave the house. I didn't want my boys to see their mom like I had to see mine at the hands of *my* father. But all I wanted to do was... *hurt* her... for getting knocked up by this guy."

"Do you know who it is? Or how long it's been going on?"

Hanging his head in shame, "I didn't even *know* it was going on."

Weston knew at that point he'd been a disgrace as a husband and had not been paying enough attention to his home because he'd been spending so much additional time outside of it. Time that was mostly allotted to Claudia while he claimed to be at work, with friends, or basically anywhere else. Naturally, that would leave open time for a woman who felt neglected and alone to seek out willing companionship.

"I haven't said anything yet to her about it. I want to ensure that there's no possible way that baby could be mine before I confront her with the vasectomy."

"You realize she's gonna be pissed that you had a surgery that affected your family's future and didn't consult with her, right?"

"Absolutely. But she fucking went out and got pregnant by someone else. That *bitch* was literally planning to pass off a baby as mine that likely isn't," he hissed.

Claudia's eyes enlarged as she stared at him. She'd never heard Weston speak that aggressively about his wife or anyone, for that matter.

"Sorry," he said, placing his hand on her thigh. "I'm just really out of sorts right now and not okay."

She leaned in and whispered in his ear, "I can make you feel better." Completely forgetting about the recent installation, Claudia's new security system captured, in great detail, her placing a patio chair cushion on the floor and dropping to her knees to orally service Weston. What also seemed to improve his mood was taking her from behind against the railing of that deck. The couples' desperate moans and animalistic screams as their bodies collided into one another rivaled the relentless whines of the cicadas. Just some additional benefits to living in a secluded area where there was no one around for miles to see or hear anything... or so they thought...

*****

The next morning, a hand riskily slid through the closing elevator doors. As they stopped and re-opened, Detective Tanner Lockhart stood ready to jump on.

"Claudia! Hey..."

"Hey," she replied meekly, still incredibly embarrassed about the scene she caused when she had accused him, but still trusting no one.

"How are you? I've been calling you. Just wanted to make sure you were okay."

"I am, thank you," she replied, avoiding eye contact.

"I just wanted to apologize again for any confusion, I hope we can still-"

The elevator doors opening and Claudia swiftly rushing out interrupted the completion of his sentence.

She approached her desk to find Lainey there waiting with a huge smile. "Missed you, partner."

Claudia rolled her eyes and offered a slight smile taking a seat at her desk. "I'm gonna need coffee."

"Damn right you will. The M.E. sent over the report last night. DNA on the second foot came back as a match to Adam Holsinger. So, whoever lured him from his car that night probably did this. Officers are on their way to the wife's house now to make the notification," Lainey said. "Oh, and the transcript came back from Linguistics. They were able to read a small portion of what Adam was yelling to the other car. But it wasn't so helpful," Lainey said, passing the typed document to Claudia.

She skimmed through the transcript which mostly consisted of Adam swearing at the unsub, trying to figure out why the driver was tailgating him with high beams.

"Well, at least we know how he's getting them to pull over. What about the hand?"

"Still waiting for DNA, but we've begun cross-referencing any domestic calls that our officers responded to with recent missing persons reports. That way, we can at least narrow down the comparison list."

"Perfect. How many have we got?"

"So, about that. As of right now, there are four missing persons reports involving men in the past two weeks, one as recently as two days ago. One is an elderly gentleman, which we can rule out because the hand isn't that old. The most recent is a Black gentleman which we can also rule out since the hand came from a Caucasian male. That leaves two, but neither was involved in any domestic disputes," Lainey explained.

"So, whoever this hand belongs to hasn't been reported missing... yet."

"My question is, how are these men even being killed and where *are* they?" Lainey questioned, standing up to lean on the side of her desk closer to Claudia. "The only pieces we have are the ones he's wanted us to find. Tox screens keep coming back negative, so we know they aren't being injected with anything – well, nothing traceable anyway. Grown-ass men don't just disappear, so where the hell are the bodies?"

14

I have the bodies. I am the piece keeper... so many pieces. Normally, I would dispose of the remainder of this particular body as I've done all the others, but I feel like having a little more fun with this one. He deserves it after what he did to that little girl. He took pieces of her, now I've got pieces of him - literally.

Years ago, I took someone he loved just to make him suffer even more. Made it look like a tragic accident. Even all those years ago, it was like I was suited for this line of work. I even attended the funeral seated near the family and watched the grief eat through him and destroy his spirit. It was beautiful... but that's the least of what he deserved. Did it make me feel better? Sure. But watching him take his final breath made me feel even more gratified. When I give him back to his family in pieces, this circle will be complete.

As I stroll out back to gather a few blocks of wood and kindling in preparation for my weekly roaring blaze, I reminisce about the amazing bonfires I used to have with friends surrounding my homemade fire pit. I made it myself. These hands are capable of far more than neatly dismembering an entire human body before a pizza delivery can even arrive.

These days, the inferno is simply part of a standard operating procedure after each outing. The victims' clothing and belongings must be properly disposed of somewhere, and the crackling fire seems most appropriate. Something also must be done with the items used to transport the pieces of these horrible people. That sweet-tailed detective was adorable barking orders to collect all the trash, thinking I would be stupid enough to leave my items anywhere they could get their nosey hands on them. So into the fire go the gloves, plastic bags, and anything else that will burn away to nothingness.

I do miss having company, though. But I can't risk guests roaming around and stumbling across Clem Rossi's arm or Kyle Larson's squishy torso. They don't even know he's missing yet, so that would simply ruin the party. And then I'd have to kill them too. Who has that kind of time? Plus, then I would have no one to send Christmas cards to.

Siiigh... It is a beautiful night for a fire, though. But something is missing. As I troll the sparsely wooded area, there it is! It's perfect! Pointy... Smooth... This will definitely do some damage. I sit back down, stare at the sharp rod, then stab it... deep... right through the marshmallow. Not nearly as gratifying as digging into human flesh, but I'm certain it will taste better.

15

As the sun rose on the first day of another year of life, Claudia's routine didn't change. Though everything seemed peaceful enough, she still walked the interior perimeter of her split-level home, looking through each window and surveying the property. When she made it to the window beside Joffrey's tank, she peeked in on him swimming alone and shook her head wondering if maybe a dog would be a better option as a pet. Hell, any dog she could get would be much less vicious than that fish.

Calls and texts delivering birthday wishes were slowly rolling in. It made Claudia think back to her childhood when her mother would always put a candle in her favorite yellow cupcake with white whipped icing, and sing Happy Birthday to her first thing in the morning. Once, when finances were tight and she wasn't able to get the cupcakes, she put a candle in a pack of ho-hos and sang to her. Those memories brought a smile to Claudia's face.

The one call she *did* take was from Hope and her nephews singing off-key to her before they left for camp. Claudia hadn't told Hope about everything that happened the night of the surprise gathering because she didn't want to worry her. So they just talked about everything else on her commute to work.

As soon as Claudia made it to the Steamy Bean counter, Levar already had her drink ready with her favorite pastry bagged up, as he had promised.

"That'll be $12.46," the cashier requested.

"It's on me," Levar replied. "Today's her birthday, y'all!" he announced loudly, unaware that Claudia hated being the center of attention.

Staff and customers around her began to wish her happy birthday, and she could feel her face heating and flushing with embarrassment.

"While I appreciate that, I can't keep letting you pay for my drinks, besides I need another coffee for a co-worker, so I'll pay for it. Medium black coffee, please."

As Levar dropped the additional coffee off, wondering who it was for, Claudia inquired, "Hey, so how did you know my birthday's today?"

"Oh uhh..." Levar stammered, "The other day when you were on the phone, you mentioned it."

Claudia paused to think back, "No... I didn't."

"Oh, well... it must have been social media then."

"Hmmm..." Claudia nodded suspiciously. "Thanks for the order guys," she said to the staff as she turned to leave the store.

Levar looked around nervously as he wiped his sweaty palms on his apron.

"Oh hey," she turned back toward him as she grabbed some extras for the coffee. "Were you there? At the bar the night of my party?" she asked, trying to play it cool and not arouse suspicion.

He paused, shook his head, then slowly answered, "No."

"Hmmm... Okay." She faked a grateful smile and continued on her way out of the coffee shop.

*****

"Teddyyy!" Claudia sang. "As promised, I got something for ya," she said, setting the piping hot coffee on the elevated desk.

"Awww... Two creams, one sugar?"

"Just how you like it..."

"You're the best! But I should be buying *you* coffee. Happy birthday. There's something here for you. Was delivered early this mornin'."

Claudia instantly felt queasy and began to look around, "What is it?" she asked, setting her coffee down on the desk.

Teddy sat before her a pale pink box perfectly wrapped with white string and a Gigi's Cupcakes sticker in the corner. She looked around again. "Do you uhh, did you see who delivered this?" she asked doing her best to mask the anxiety in her voice, but clearly failing.

No one knew about the annual birthday cupcake other than her, her deceased mother, and her incarcerated stepfather. She did mention it in therapy. *Could it be from Dr. Pearce? Eh, that would probably be inappropriate.*

"Nope. It just came via one of those bike couriers. White guy, hat, sunglasses. He didn't need a signature. He just sat it on the desk. Said it was for you."

"So he was *carrying* it?"

"Well not exactly, it was in a clear bag. He slid the sides of the bag down and gestured for me to take it so I... took it," Teddy chuckled not realizing the gravity of the situation. "But I can smell it through the box. Smells great! Let me know how it tastes," he said cheerily.

Knowing she had no intention of eating that cupcake, Claudia simply smiled and picked the box up by the corners, using only the tip of her middle finger and thumb. She was already positive that if the same person who murdered those men had anything to do with this cupcake, they were not going to find any prints other than Teddy's, but she would send it off to the lab anyway just in case.

On the elevator ride up, she thought maybe she was simply overreacting, and possibly Lainey left it as a surprise, knowing how much Claudia loves sweets. *Duh, Lainey wouldn't have it delivered when she's coming here.*

When she made it to her desk, Claudia gently set the perfect pink box down.

"Ooooh, Gigi's! That's a pretty pricey cupcake you got there, who's it from?" Lainey nosily inquired. "Happy birthday, by the way!"

"Thank you," Claudia replied, now distracted as she quickly put on a pair of the black disposable gloves they all kept in their desks. She reached for her scissors to delicately cut the corded string that held the box closed, then slowly opened it to reveal the most perfect lavender lemon cupcake she'd ever seen. The smell was intoxicating and immediately caught the attention of nearby colleagues.

"Wow is that stunning," Lainey gushed. "But why the gloves?"

"This was just left at the front desk... No name, nothing."

"Could it be from your *friend* a few doors down?"

"I don't think so. I don't think he would pay a bike courier to drop something off when he works two doors down. Though he did lie to me about being at the bar last week."

"Seriously?" Lainey asked. "He was there? He didn't talk to you or anything?"

"No... though I'm wondering if he's the one who sent the drink."

"I'll call over and see what kind of video footage Frank has in that place. See if we notice anything strange."

"Thanks."

"I'll also check out the video surveillance footage outside of the precinct and see if anything pops. Rookie!"

"I have a name," Detective Lockhart replied.

"I know, *rookie*."

Even though it may not have been his fault, Lainey was still annoyed with him from the birthday events that transpired the week prior. "Pull up the surveillance cam footage from outside the station for this week. I'm gonna pull up last week's. We're looking for anyone suspicious, any one person who's lingering around - blue jacket guy maybe... from the crime scene photos?"

Claudia thanked her colleagues and continued packaging the box containing the sweet pastry into an evidence bag to deliver to the crime lab.

Laura was more than willing to see if they could find any prints or trace evidence on the box or toxins in the cupcake. However, based on the lack of evidence previously collected, she wasn't optimistic. But a person can only be stellar for so long. Eventually, there has to be a slip.

Upon her arrival back to the station, Lainey immediately summoned Claudia over. "Hey! Spoke to Frank who said his only cameras are pointed at the bar's cash registers, so that's no help, but look at this! So last week, when you were leaning against the squad car talking on the phone, there's Levar, right?"

"Right. But I knew he was there. I spoke to him after the call."

"Right, but look across the street. This same guy's out there almost every day on a laptop."

Claudia pulled up different still images that showed the same light-skinned man lingering around the station. It was almost always toward the end of Claudia's work day, but sometimes in the afternoon, as well. On days when she would work later than usual, he would eventually leave.

He just blends in with the crowd. There's literally nothing special about him that would call him to anyone's immediate attention. Average height, average build.

"Pull up Blue Jacket from the crime scenes and see if this guy matches. It could be him."

Claudia stood speechless and queasy watching Lainey pull up all this footage of a man who had clearly been following her. She wasn't going crazy. But there was a bigger problem that turned Claudia's face ashen. Lainey asked, "What's wrong?"

"I think he's outside... right now," Claudia replied with her hand on her stomach. "Across the street. I think I passed him on my way in from the crime lab."

"What?" Lainey pulled up the live cam footage, and sure enough, he was comfortably seated at one of the café tables with a cup of coffee, a notepad, and a pen.

Lainey immediately sprung from her seat, summoning three other detectives.

"If he tries to run, I want coverage from every angle. Carlson, you take the right. Lockhart, I want you to swing around behind him. Torrey, you take the left. I will approach him directly from the front. If this is the guy who's murdering people and stalking one of ours, he may be armed. Do *not* let him get away. Burgess, you're with me," Lainey ordered.

"What about me? I'm coming too!" Claudia demanded.

"You're staying put. We don't know what his deal is."

They immediately took off, but Claudia followed them down the stairs and stayed inside the station, watching through the large glass windows and doors.

She and Teddy waited anxiously as Detectives Crane and Burgess approached the unsuspecting man. He stood and removed his sunglasses to talk to them. But then out of nowhere, he threw his cup of hot coffee at Burgess and took off running to the left where Torrey was waiting in the wings. The man stopped abruptly when he saw the detective draw his weapon. As he looked around and saw he was surrounded by guns aimed at him, he finally put his hands up.

"We weren't coming out here to arrest you. We just wanted to talk," Lainey reprimanded. "But when you throw hot coffee on my colleague, *now* that's assault, so we're gonna do a little more than talk," she said while a wet and furious Detective Burgess handcuffed him.

As they walked him through the station's glass doors, they stopped when they unexpectedly saw Claudia standing with Teddy in the lobby. Relief washed over her knowing that they finally had a suspect in custody.

As they proceeded toward the elevators, Claudia stared into his brown eyes when he passed her. He looked so familiar, like she'd known him her entire life but couldn't place from where. It also hit her that he was the same person outside of her therapy appointment that day. Dr. Pearce was right when she said it could be someone she sees often but doesn't really *notice*. How many times was he in her periphery while she was out getting coffee or leaving work and he was just blending in with the background unnoticeably? Had he been lingering around in stores with her? Had he followed her home? She squeezed her eyes closed, trying so hard to recollect why this man would look so familiar to her, but nothing came.

16

Claudia entered the observation room where the captain and the other detectives involved were watching Lainey talk to the gentleman through the two-way mirror.

"So they think he's a match to Blue Jacket," Captain Higgins said to Claudia.

"Who *is* he?"

"His name is Isaiah Mills, 29 years old. They ran his prints and he doesn't have any priors; he's not in the system."

They watched in silence as the interrogation began.

"Mr. Mills, I'm Detective Lainey Crane, and you remember Detective Eric Burgess? The one you wanted to share your coffee with? Can I ask why you've been outside of our station almost every day recently?"

"I am just there to have coffee. Sometimes I work. That is not a crime."

"So you're saying it's *not* because you've been following one of our detectives?"

He didn't reply.

"Okay." Lainey laid out two images of a man who clearly visibly matched this guy's description at the crime scenes. "Is this you?"

He glanced down at the images but still didn't reply.

"Okay." Lainey nodded then laid out three more images of body parts in front of him, "Did you do this?"

He looked at the images and pushed himself back from the table, "What!? Oh nooo, I did *not* do that!"

With not even a prior traffic ticket, Lainey could buy that. How often does someone go from having zero trouble with the law *ever*, to killing and dismembering three grown men? Besides, he didn't appear to fit Weston's profile, in addition to the fact that only about fifteen percent of serial killers are Black. But that doesn't mean he wasn't tailing her partner.

"Fine," Lainey said as she scooped up all the pictures and put them back in the folder. "So we don't need you to confirm it. We know it's you in these images. What *I* need to know is why you were at all of Detective Martinez's active crime scenes? Why are you stalking her?"

"Stalking? No. I- I don't know," Isaiah faltered. "I just wanted to... see her in action I guess..."

"That kinda sounds like stalking to me," she interrupted. "You're seated across from her workplace... regularly. We have you on surveillance... following her to appointments... crime scenes. You expect us to believe that you're not the one who sent that pink box to this office today? And hey... tell me why you killed her fish. The mystery is just plaguing me."

Isaiah's eyes widened as the detective hurled multiple accusations at him, one after another, "I am *not* stalking anyone. I have just been trying to work up the nerve to... talk to her. And I definitely did not *kill* any fish!" he declared as if that were the weirdest thing he'd ever heard.

Claudia watched this man's facial expressions and body movements that all continued to look exceedingly familiar, but she still could not place this person.

"Well, I'm sorry to inform you," Lainey replied patronizingly, "but you're a little young for her. Almost positive you're not her type."

"What? I'm not trying to sleep with her! Ew!" he exclaimed, turning up his nose.

The eyebrows of everyone listening shot up in disbelief, including Lainey's, because "Ew" is the very last word that any of them would use to describe Detective Martinez.

"I'm... I am her... brother... And I need her help."

Everyone in the observation room turned their attention to Claudia in disbelief.

"I don't have a brother," she stammered in confused disbelief before storming out of the observation room.

"Well, unless her sister had a very convincing gender reassignment surgery in the last 72 hours, Detective Martinez doesn't *have* a brother," Lainey countered.

"Except, she does."

Claudia angrily burst through the interrogation room door and slammed her hand down on the metal table. "Who the fuck are you, *really*? I don't have a brother!"

Lainey jumped up and pulled her back from the table.

"Miles Evans is our father."

"That *murderer* is *not* my father. And you being one of his many illegitimate children does *not* make you my brother!"

"He is not a murderer!" Isaiah stood up and yelled back. Burgess positioned his tall sturdy frame in between him and the detectives. "He didn't kill our mother!!"

Our mother. Claudia jaggedly exhaled the breath she had been holding as Lainey grabbed hold of her and maneuvered her out of the interrogation room into the hall as the door closed behind them.

Lainey kept hold of Claudia to make sure she was okay after what she'd just heard. The captain joined them.

"Is that true?" he asked.

"My mother was pregnant when she died. No one told me… I thought the baby died too. Why wouldn't anyone tell me that I had a sibling?" Quickly composing herself, "I'll talk to him."

"Wait wait, are you sure that's a good idea? Are you sure you can handle this?"

"Well if he's been following me all this time, he clearly wants to talk to *me*, so his guard will be down. Who better to get the information from him?"

Lockhart handed her two bottles of water to take in with her. She flinched slightly when he got close enough to slide a clear plastic bag into her blazer pocket.

As Claudia slowly re-entered the room, Isaiah stood up to greet her, as any gentleman should when a lady arrives. But Burgess stepped forward, still on guard, not knowing if it was manners or impending aggression. Claudia gave him a nod that it was okay for him to stand down, so he left the room. She set the bottle of water on the table in front of Isaiah and took a seat across from him.

"Thank you... for the water. And for talking to me."

She nodded as she opened her water and took a nice long gulp in hopes that he would follow suit, which he did. Now they would at least have his exact DNA in the event that they found something to compare it to.

It all made sense now why he looked so incredibly familiar. He actually very much resembled *her*. Claudia looked like her mother and so did her brother, except he was built like his father, minus the portly midsection, which was sure to arrive by middle age. His build, the mannerisms, even his gait - all Miles. But the fairer skin tone, warm brown eyes, and entire dental structure, all belonged to their mother, Janet.

"I am truly sorry. I did not mean to scare you. I just was trying to figure out the best way to approach you. I- I didn't know if you knew about me or not... Clearly, you did not."

Claudia listened quietly.

"I was hesitant to just pop up on you in the street and be like, 'Heyyy, guess what? You have a brother!'"

"You *do* understand that would have been a better scenario than this one, right?"

He nodded and smiled which made Claudia melt a little inside because it was like seeing her mother smile back at her.

The officers in the observation room listened as he told Claudia about how after he was born, he was placed with a Caucasian family in an affluent part of town. While it is usually the preference of Children and Youth Services to place children with parents of the same race, there was a shortage of Black or Hispanic families back then to take children. CYS had to have known that they were siblings, and she couldn't help but wonder why they wouldn't have asked her adoptive family to take her brother.

"It wasn't until a few years ago that my adoptive family told me the truth about our father... *my* father," he quickly corrected, "being incarcerated for killing our mom."

Claudia listened to him talk and it made sense to her that he had been raised in that predominantly Caucasian area. To be a Black/Hispanic man, he had very little urban tone to his voice, with even less urban appeal and swag. He was especially proper, barely even using contractions let alone any slang, even while conversing with her. It was almost as if he had no idea what code-switching was.

"Of course, trusty Google," he continued, "I looked everything up and read about the trial and saw you as a child. So then I set out to find you, which was relatively easy because your name is everywhere in the press solving cases and whatnot. So I thought maybe you would be able to help."

"Are you in some sorta trouble?"

"No... not me, my dad... He did not do this."

Claudia closed her eyes while he yammered on and her breathing became slightly uneven listening to that foolishness when she knew damn well that man pushed her pregnant mother down a flight of steps. She was there.

"I have visited him in prison... many times. He still maintains, to this day, that he did *not* do it. I thought maybe, as a detective... If you could just re-look at the case file... there have been more advancements in testing, maybe you could find something that would exonerate him."

She felt her entire face twitch.

"Maybe if you just went to see him and spoke to him yourself," Isaiah begged. "He's had you on his visitation list all this time. You could look him in the eyes and see that he is actually telling the truth."

Her eyes narrowed as she leaned into him. In a hushed tone that only the two of them could hear, she replied, "I will do no such thing. I have no interest in seeing let alone exonerating your trash murderer father. Stay the *fuck* away from me. If I see you again, I'll make sure you end up in there *with* him for some *real* father-son bonding. Do you understand?" He recoiled looking into her dark, angry stare.

She took a sip of her water, calmly exhaled, and sat back in her seat. Her brother was silent, avoiding eye contact with her and staring desperately at the glass wall wondering if anyone back there heard what she said to him. But she knew they hadn't. Claudia tapped on the mirror. "We're done here."

As Burgess escorted Isaiah Mills out of the interrogation room to process him for the assault charge, she pulled out a disposable glove and the baggie, then carefully placed the bottled water inside to deliver to the crime lab.

*****

Claudia anxiously paced between her living room and dining room in her oversized men's button-down dress shirt and pink boy shorts. Her curls bounced loosely over her shoulders with every step. *What do I say? Like how do I approach this? Okay, you know what? Just do it. Make the call.*

She dialed the number but as it started to ring she quickly hung up and continued nervously pacing until the phone vibrated in her hand and startled her.

"Hi..."

"Hey sis, I saw I missed your call," Hope cheerily replied. "What's up? You okay?"

"Yeah, I uh..." Claudia paused and then exhaled realizing that there was no real way to beat around this bush. "So I met my brother today," she quickly blurted out, then immediately wished she would've been more tactful.

"Your *what*??"

"Yep, I was just as surprised as you. His name is Isaiah. Apparently, my mom died but the baby somehow made it?" she replied, cozying up in her oversized armchair.

"Awww, CoCo..."

"You were much older than me, did you know anything about this? I mean I can't ask *our* mom now..."

Hope paused to think, "I do remember overhearing our parents talk once about whether or not they should take in another baby, so that must have been your brother. It was *very* shortly after you came to be with us."

"Well, why didn't they? He's my brother. Nobody wanted to keep us together? Or even mention it to me?"

"I mean, I'm sure some of it had to do with their financial stability. Adding another child to the family is expensive enough, then you add an infant on top of that? Plus, you had *just* arrived and I feel like honestly, they didn't want to take away any of the attention that *you* needed."

Claudia quietly processed what her sister was saying, which made sense. But she wished she could just talk to their mother, who was no longer with them. Neither of the girls dealt well with the aneurysm that took her to be with their late father a few years ago.

"Plus, you had essentially just lost both of your parents and with me going off to college just a couple years later, I sensed that they wanted to be able to give you the full devotion of two parents that you lost, but deserved."

"They *were* pretty great parents," Claudia smiled thinking of how loving and supportive the Jacobs were and how they treated her like their own.

"They *so* were!" Hope replied with a smile in her voice. "Do you remember that backyard camping adventure?"

Claudia laughed, "I'm convinced that's the reason I never became a girl scout! Those woods were scary!"

"Woods? It was *three* trees," Hope laughed. "We lived in the freaking suburbs, drama queen! *Your* thick woods are way scarier!"

Their laughter died down and Claudia shifted back to the original topic. "So you don't know why they never even mentioned him? I mean, he grew up not far from us. There could have at least been playdates or visitations... something. Like, anything so that my only biological family and I didn't grow up adopted thinking we were alone."

"I don't disagree with you, CoCo. The only thing I could think of is possibly your therapist? Maybe she recommended not to? I remember them arguing because this doctor was so expensive. But she was supposed to be the best."

"You mean Dr. Marx? The one we saw after Rico passed away?"

"No, we saw her briefly but you were then referred to someone else. I don't remember his name though."

Claudia began pacing between the two rooms staring at her phone in confusion. She racked her brain trying to think back so long ago, but she only remembered Dr. Marx and then the therapist she saw throughout college.

"You don't remember him? At all? You saw him for over a year."

"Ohhh... yeah," Claudia played it off. "I remember now," she replied even though she absolutely didn't. How could an entire person just disappear from her memory?

"So are you okay? What happened? Did he just want to reconnect? Or does he need a kidney or something? You know family comes out the woodwork when they need organs."

Claudia chuckled. "No. He said he'd been in contact with Miles and that he maintains his innocence. Wants *me* to help him clear his name. Can you believe that?"

"Holy Snickers!"

"Hope, you're an adult. You're allowed to swear."

"Habit. I'm tellin' you that damn baby repeats everything I say. I wasn't ready for this level of censorship when I had kids. Last week, we were getting' out the car and I was on the phone with a friend. My response to her was, 'biiitch, please.' That little punk said 'biiitch, pease' all through Walmart. I was mortified! Every person we passed, he would wave, throw them that adorable smile of his, and as soon as they would wave back, he would say, 'biiitch, pease, biiitch, pease.'"

Claudia laughed uncontrollably. She really needed that release. "And you want me to have one of those? If I wanted to deal with that shit, I would just get a parrot."

Hope released a long sigh, "So... did you tell Isaiah no?"

"I think so," Claudia replied rubbing her fingers through her soft tresses.

"You *think* so?"

"I mean yeah, I definitely... told him no. He wanted me to go to the prison and *see* him! Do you know how hard it was to maintain my composure and not laugh in his face?"

"So just to quickly play devil's advocate here, have you ever actually looked at your mother's case file?"

"No, why would I? Miles pushed her, I saw him, she died, he was convicted, the end..."

"Okay, well… just be careful. I don't want anything to happen to you, CoCo."

"Biiitch, pease!" she joked, mocking her nephew. "I'll be fine. Love you."

"Love you back!"

And with that, they ended the call. Claudia sat in her oversized plush chair in silence trying to figure out how a past therapist completely went missing from her memory.

17

"We have combed through so much video footage and there's literally nothing. It's like this perp is a ghost. I'm seriously beginning to wonder if Weston's profile is off," Lainey expressed. "The way this unsub is able to either disable or avoid cameras, leave body parts with little to no trace evidence... I just feel like this person has to have a more extensive knowledge of the city's surveillance system than was noted in the profile."

"When we get the report back regarding the third victim, we can send that over to Weston to see if he needs to amend it," Claudia replied.

A phone call from Laura interrupted her skimming through the digitized files of her mother's case from almost thirty years ago. From what Claudia could quickly see, there was nothing that looked out of place that would indicate that Miles was not guilty of the crime committed. But she would surely need to spend some additional time when she could focus more on that particular task.

"So..." Claudia said, hanging up her phone, "The cupcake was clean. No toxins and the only prints on the outside of the cupcake box were mine and Teddy's. This means the box had to have been wiped down because, at the very least, there should have been a few more sets of prints."

"Right, I've been to Gigi's. Those boxes are already assembled along the back wall and there are always multiple people working. So there should be at least one if not two, additional sets of randomly placed prints all over that box."

"Exactly," Claudia replied. "Laura said they even tried to pull prints from the outside of the cupcake wrapper, but there were none. I'm guessing because staff puts on a glove before handling the pastries."

"Okay, but that's good!"

Claudia looked confused. "How is that helpful?"

"I mean, not good for the case, but good that they're following rules and being cleanly and conscientious. I feel even better eating the cupcakes now."

"I'm done with you, Lainey."

Claudia slammed her pen on the desk, stood up, and began pacing. "Ugh! They have no video surveillance inside the shop and we don't know *when* the cupcake was even purchased. They sell easily three dozen of just *that* flavor alone, daily! It could be anyone." She began to pick at her cuticles as she let out a long exasperated sigh. "I'm tired. Frustrated and tired."

"Well you can't be too tired yet," Lainey replied, looking at her computer. "Captain! The M.E. just sent over the report," she announced.

Higgins made his way over to the group as Lainey continued, "So the owner of the hand found at The Point is Kyle Larson. Age forty-two. He was already in the system - served time for a string of burglaries and random drug charges."

Tanner commented, "Ya know, I've said it before and I'll say it again. I seriously think we should let this perp keep doin' his thing because he's just cleaning up for us."

Everyone within earshot looked at him only to realize he wasn't joking. Tanner continued, "What? We are quite literally only finding pieces of *bad* people," he said, plopping into his chair causing it to roll back a bit. He continued, "I mean, you know how hard it is for abuse victims to get out, so I'm just sayin' this unsub is *helping*. I'm with Elsa on this one – Let it Go."

Claudia chuckled inside because she didn't completely disagree, but she needed to get these folks back on track. "So there's no missing persons report for Kyle Larson?"

"Not yet. It's been about a week."

"Did we get a 9-1-1 call for his residence?" Captain Higgins asked.

After quickly doing a database search, Claudia answered, "No, his address isn't appearing in any of these records."

"That's not right. Every one of these guys was involved in a 9-1-1 call," Higgins observed, opening his pack of cigarettes and removing one.

"But what about that call in the park two weeks ago?" Tanner interjected.

"Oh yeah," Burgess agreed. "Good memory, rookie. Pittsburgh PD's been looping us in on domestic calls since this whole thing started. They responded to a domestic incident at the park where a man had grabbed his girlfriend by the hair and forcefully slammed her to the ground." Tanner pulled up the report while Burgess continued the story. "Multiple witnesses called 9-1-1, but when officers arrived on the scene, a few minutes later, he had already fled. She refused to press charges or even give them his name. We ended up finding it in her social media account."

"And I take it no cameras in the park?"

"Of course not. That would make too much sense," Burgess replied with a sarcastic chuckle.

Tanner handed the report to Lainey, "The girlfriend's name is Amber Monroe and they have a six-year-old daughter, Paisley."

"Make the notification and see if you can find anything else out," the captain ordered as he made his way to the exit to get a few puffs in.

*****

The detectives waited on the porch for the door to finally open. "Amber Monroe?"

"Yes?" she answered warily through a slightly cracked door.

"I'm Detective Martinez and this is Detective Crane. May we come in, please?"

"I'd rather you not."

"That's fine." The detectives exchanged looks before continuing. "Our officers responded to a call in the park the other day regarding your boyfriend, Kyle Larson. When was the last time you saw him?"

"Um... That day in the park. He ran away when he heard the police coming. He- he didn't mean to hurt me."

"That's not what we got from the witnesses."

"Well, they're *wrong*! They don't know *him* and they don't know *us*!" Amber yelled defensively. "He's a good guy. He just... has a little bit of a temper is all. But he's workin' on it."

"So that's why you didn't press charges? Because he's *workin'* on it?" Claudia asked, trying her best to keep the disdain out of her voice.

"I just... didn't want him to get in trouble again. He already has two strikes. Plus, I love him and I can't deal with him going to jail again."

"So you haven't heard from him since then?"

"He called to apologize later that night and was supposed to come over the next day to talk, but he never did. His phone went straight to voicemail when I called to see if he was still coming."

"So if he never showed up, and you haven't heard from him since, why didn't you report him missing?"

"Well, I guess I didn't think that he was actually missing. Just figured he was being an asshole and avoiding us again." Amber glanced back and forth between the two detectives. "Is he okay? Do you know where he's at? Paisley keeps asking for him and I'm making up excuses for his absence - again."

"We're sorry to have to inform you, but Kyle Larson has been involved in a... situation that leads us to believe that he's no longer... alive," Lainey responded.

The detectives watched what color there was drain from Amber's already pale face as she backed up into her apartment. Claudia stepped into the home just in time to catch Amber as she fell crying into her arms.

"Is Paisley in school right now?"

"Yes," Amber replied between sobs.

"Okay, that's good. May we sit?"

Amber nodded, still sobbing as Claudia guided her into her living room, where they spent the next half-hour trying their best to explain what the investigators thought had happened to Kyle.

"Well, that was intense," Lainey remarked as they stepped off Amber's porch, heading toward the car. "How much you wanna bet that we also won't be able to track his cell phone number because the phone has been disabled or destroyed?"

"I can't take that bet because you're probably right. But we can at least get his last known location."

"The crazy part is that she was so worried about him going to jail, but had Kyle been apprehended that day, he might still be alive."

Claudia thought to herself, *and still beating Amber's ass*, but she just nodded in agreement with Lainey's statement as they got into the car.

"Hey, wanna grab a coffee on the way back in?" Lainey asked.

"Sure, don't I always?" Claudia answered, fiddling with her sleeves.

18

Emma slept in for a change, rolling over to embrace the man who should have been lying beside her, but that half of the bed was cold and empty the past few mornings. With a sigh, she got up and engaged in her normal morning routine that involved a shower, a K-Cup, and watching talk shows while also glancing out the window to make sure the children, while awaiting their school buses, were not damaging the lawn. Her husband put so much work into that front yard in what little spare time he had.

She saw her neighbor walking up the driveway, so Emma met her at the door. Her sparkling green eyes lit up. "Linda! Good morning, doll. Come on in," she said as she opened the door wider and stepped away so her friend could enter.

Linda bent down to pick up a box before stepping into the house, "Well, what've we got here?"

Emma turned back around to find her holding a long purple and black box that read "Micah's Florals" embossed in shiny gold lettering. "Oh my word, I didn't even notice that there," she said with a bashful smile.

"It was upright, leaned against the side of the door," Linda said, handing Emma the box. "You know you're the envy of all the wives, right? Your husband is always doing something sweet to romance you. Mine hasn't done anything romantic since the day he proposed over forty years ago," she complained with an eye roll.

Linda was correct in her assessment. Emma's husband was always incredibly nurturing and hopelessly romantic when it came to her. Flowers came often, as did impromptu date nights, expensive gifts, and vacations. He had always treated her like a queen. After they tragically lost their daughter years ago, they weren't sure the marriage would survive either. But they persevered choosing to love and focus on each other every day. After all, neither of them was at fault for her accident.

Emma chuckled as she set the box down on the kitchen island.

"So the reason I'm here, you know Roger and I recently renovated the basement and turned it into an in-home theater."

"Well see, that's sweet, right?"

"Please. He did that for himself so he could watch football on the largest possible screen ever. But what some of us *ladies* would prefer to view on that large screen is something more exciting than sweaty men pummeling each other."

"Well, what's more exciting than that?" Emma asked, sipping her hazelnut coffee with a naughty smirk.

"*Magic Mike* on a screen the size of that wall right there," she giggled. "They have a third movie out, so I figured this would be a great time for a refresher so we can prepare for the next, right? It's like research. Scholarly, educational research of... the human anatomy."

"I agree. Education is, after all, one of the many keys to success," she remarked teasingly. "When does this tutelage take place?" she asked with a haughty accent, extending her pinky finger for dramatic effect.

"Friday. Right after I get my grandson on the bus and the other husbands leave for work, we are meeting at my place and I'll have all the movie theater goodies available. Popcorn, nachos, candy, wine, you name it."

"Perfect. Count me in. Ugh, where are my manners? Would you like some coffee?"

"Oh, no thank you," Linda replied, turning toward the door. "I've got to run; the landscaper should be here within the next half hour or so, and he works topless," she winked. "Goodness knows *my* husband's not going to do it like yours does. Oh, but wait! I need to see these flowers," she said, strolling back toward the kitchen area.

"Oh yes!" Emma replied, setting her coffee down next to the box to grab a pair of scissors.

"I need to live vicariously through you since the last time I got flowers from my husband was after his second affair. *Bastard.*"

Emma just shook her head, unsure of how to respond because she wouldn't have stayed with her husband after a *first* affair, let alone a second. And in her mind, if there was a second, there was probably a third or fourth that simply hadn't been discovered yet. But she didn't have the heart to say that to her friend. And it probably wouldn't matter much anyway because she'd told the ladies that the love was gone and she was only there for the money at that point.

Emma continued cutting through the ribbon and tape on the side of the box as her neighbor nosily peeked in.

"Oh my gosh!" Emma whispered with her hand over her mouth.

"Oooooh, it's something exotic, isn't it?" Linda asked excitedly, hopping back and forth on her toes like an excited five-year-old. "He's always had phenomenal taste!"

"Oh my *gosh*!" Emma voiced a little louder stepping backward, accidentally taking the coffee with her. The mug shattered onto the floor and she screamed as piping hot coffee splashed onto her bare feet.

Linda immediately ran around the island and grabbed the hand towel to assist but stopped in her tracks when she noticed that the box did not appear to contain flowers.

Emma leaned against the back counter using the refrigerator for stability as she cried out, while Linda continued to make her way toward the box. When her mind finally adjusted to seeing what was inside, she screamed and jumped back as well to hold her friend in her arms.

*****

Claudia jumped when her hip began vibrating. She answered it on speakerphone.

"Hey Captain, we-"

"Code 3. I need you to head over to 1674 Cordell Dr.," he interrupted. Claudia quietly gasped when she heard the address. "We've got another situation. This one's going to bring *way* more attention and pressure."

"We're about fifteen minutes out," Lainey replied.

Reds and blues flickered quickly as they made a quick and mildly reckless U-turn. Claudia remained silent, breathing deeply, listening to the air enter and exit her body as she stared aimlessly out of the passenger window. The captain's announcement kept replaying in her mind, *Code 3* - the code that indicates to proceed immediately with lights and sirens. So whatever they were going to find there was not going to be good.

As she nervously picked at her fingernails, Claudia could hear Lainey talking to her but she couldn't make out the words. It was like another bad dream from which she was just waiting, no *trying*, to jolt herself awake.

As they pulled onto Cordell, Claudia observed all of the extravagant homes when they passed by each one, eventually pulling up to 1674. Lainey placed her hand on Claudia's thigh and asked, "Hey, what's goin' on? Are you okay?"

"Yeah, I'm okay, I just... know the people here, is all," she said despondently, exiting the car.

Officers were already on the scene as the detectives slowly approached the stunning Italianate-style Victorian mini manse. Nosy neighbors with nothing better to do had already gathered behind the yellow tape to speculate and gossip. Claudia was sure of it.

Upon entering the majestic open space, Claudia noticed the two older women, one still in tears, speaking with two officers. She glanced over to the mantle above the fireplace, then scanned the room until she made it over to the kitchen where the medical examiner was handling a box with black-gloved hands. Though she wanted to know the contents of the box, she couldn't bring herself to go over there.

Just as they made eye contact, the slim, bi-racial woman with loose greying curls ran over to her, "Ohhhh, Claudia!" she said, crying and embracing her. Colleagues in the room exchanged subtle glances wondering how the two were acquainted.

"Ms. Emma, I am *so* sorry," she said sadly but still composed.

"They said that he might be dead," she wailed between sobs. "But he could still be alive, right?" She looked to Claudia with all the hope in the world, awaiting an affirmative response. But one never came and the look of pain on Claudia's face, which she tried desperately to hide for Ms. Emma's sake, told all she needed to know.

As she wrapped her arms around Emma to comfort her, Claudia glanced up at Alessandra, who also did not offer a favorable nonverbal response to her question.

"Come on Ms. Emma, let's go over and sit back down with the officers here."

She accompanied her back to the plush ivory sectional and took a seat beside her, their hands intertwined for emotional support.

"Okay, Mrs. Walker, you were telling us why you hadn't filed a missing persons report if you hadn't seen your husband in two days," the officer reminded her.

"He was supposed to be out of town at a medical conference in California," she said, still holding Claudia's hand tightly. "I called his phone and it went to voicemail, but that wasn't uncommon. He's a surgeon... He *was* a surgeon," she answered, falling apart all over again. Once she regained a little more composure, Emma continued, "When he would go away, he would almost always call me in the mornings before his day started, but with the time difference... I didn't hear from him, so I figured the flowers were just to let me know he was thinking of me. He was *always* thinking of me," she whispered, falling into tears again.

Claudia watched as Lainey strolled the perimeter of the family room and came upon the mantel covered in an eclectic display of picture frames filled with photos taken over the years. Lainey continued sauntering the width of the six-foot fireplace taking in all the photos, then she stopped abruptly and looked over at her partner.

Claudia immediately looked away turning her attention back to the sobbing woman holding her hand.

"I'm all alone now," she cried. "First my baby girl and now my husband? I can't... you're going to catch whoever did this, right?"

"I promise. We will do our best, Ms. Emma. I will call you myself to keep you updated."

"Thank you, baby," she said, patting Claudia's hand.

Detective Martinez made her way down the back hallway until she came upon a closed door to the left. It creaked as she slowly pushed it open and entered the dimly lit office. On the wall behind his large cedar desk, situated between two floor-to-ceiling windows, hung his multiple degrees, awards, and commendations. To the left was a massive canvas painting that he had commissioned for the couple's 25th wedding anniversary. Across from that, lived an entire built-in library of medical books, in addition to a section for personal reading. Just as she was about to remove one of the books from the shelf, Lainey quietly entered the room.

"So... That photo on the mantel of you and the victim..."

"Yeah. Dr. Darrell Walker is uh," she paused, glancing solemnly around the room, "He's my biological father. Ms. Emma is my stepmother."

"Oh Claudia, I had no idea. I'm so sorry." She went to hug her, but Claudia put her hand up as if to say that's not necessary. "You don't seem too broken up about it," Lainey astutely observed.

"I mean we weren't very close, so I guess I've just developed this level of indifference where he's concerned. I don't love him or hate him – he's just the man who got my mother pregnant."

Lainey nodded in understanding because she didn't have the best relationship with her father either after coming out. But she still looked concerned for her partner.

Claudia continued, "He left my mother when she was pregnant to go off and do some medical internship and acted like we'd never happened in his life. *Clearly,*" she waved her hand toward the desk bitterly, "he went on to do great things and never thought twice about us. Then when I was three, Mom met Miles and just like that, we were a new family."

"Who's the other girl in the photos?"

"She was *their* daughter, Teena. She died a while ago, hence the shrine to her," Claudia said with the slightest eye roll, making it evident that she wasn't *quite* as indifferent as she thought she was.

"That tracks, considering the oldest she looks in any of the pictures is late teens."

"Almost eighteen. It was a freak car accident after a party. She was speeding not wearing a seatbelt, and oddly, none of the airbags deployed. So she was ejected from the vehicle."

"That's a lot of tragedy for that sweet woman out there to endure. I'm really sorry. Did you know Teena?"

"I knew *of* her. He and I didn't get reacquainted until a few years after she'd passed away. I guess I was the less desirable replacement daughter, even though *technically*, I was here first. But I was just an officer, nothing important. Teena was going to follow in his footsteps and be the next Dr. Walker. I mean, who knows? Maybe had he elected to actually raise me, *I* could have been the next Dr. Walker."

"True, but then we wouldn't have met and your life would be far less fulfilling," Lainey replied playfully trying to help lift her spirits.

"You're not wrong," Claudia chuckled.

"Why do you call her Ms. Emma?"

"It's a cultural thing, I guess. We were raised that it's disrespectful to call your elders by their first names."

Lainey nodded, "I can appreciate that."

"This is just so weird because he doesn't fit the profile of the other victims. He was never even remotely aggressive with me," Claudia murmured as she moved about the room. "I don't honestly believe he would've ever laid a hand on Ms. Emma. I mean look at her. She's out there in a tank top and Bermuda shorts. That is *not* the wardrobe of a woman who is sustaining regular physical abuse." Claudia glanced up at the striking painting of the Walkers looking adoringly into each other's eyes. "He loved that woman more than he *ever* loved me."

19

He's perfect. We can help one another. He needs something from me, and I need something from him. This poor soul is invisible to the world. People pass by him every single day and look right through him, just as they often do me. I find it mildly disturbing that I could have anything in common with the likes of him, but he'll do. Very few will notice him and no one will miss him if it comes down to it.

"You! Sir! Come here."

He has no reason not to. Despite my recent... activities, I don't appear threatening to the naked eye. Not that he'll be able to see me well anyway, as I linger in the shadow of darkness.

I watch patiently as he wheels over his well-worn grocery cart, full of his every earthly belonging. I can smell him long before he reaches me - covered in filth and facial hair, needing a shower in sixteen of the worst possible ways. But his scent and appearance are irrelevant in regard to my task at hand.

"I have a job for you."

I lift from the ground and drop into his cart three black contractor bags. His eyes widen and his mouth falls open when I hand him a stack of crisp new ten-dollar bills totaling $300.

"There are four dumpsters on this side of this alley. I would like you to leave one of these bags on top of the first three you come to."

He goes to look inside one of the bags. "DON'T! There's nothing in there you would want."

"But the bags is open. You want me to tie 'em up first? They don't smell so right."

"Leave them as they are. Do not look inside. I will be following... watching you... If my directions are not carried out completely, I will return for my money and your body will be found in the fourth dumpster."

He nods fearfully and places the thick wad in his jacket pocket.

"Oh, and if you say a word about this to anyone, anyone at all, I will kill you. Slowly. Painfully. And I will enjoy it."

I feel like I said that in my nicest possible tone, but that doesn't stop him from quickly scooting off with my deliveries. By the time he turns to see if I'm still watching him, I'm already gone making my way to another location to observe him from above.

He carries out my instructions, then immediately goes to McDonald's. I find it amusing to watch him for a portion of the night strolling through town, guard highly elevated, looking around... looking for me... like he's being watched. He is. They all are. Now to make my way across town to carry out the remainder of my evening plans.

*****

Doritos are my snack of choice as I wait and watch in darkness, with only the light of the full moon illuminating the damp street. Normally, it's a little more complex getting my new friends alone this late at night, but Joe here makes it relatively easy. All of his carousing and running the streets means he's not keeping bankers' hours. So I wait and snack, while I watch from the side street as Joe drinks himself into a stupor with his friends when he should be at home with his wife and child.

Joe is the worst kind of human. One who just really doesn't need to be here any longer. Not only is he beating on his wife, but he's also cheating on her. I just want to grab him, shake him, and say, "Joe, if you're going to dip your stick into another woman, do better than that flea-infested looking trash monger you're whoring around with."

He finally stumbles out to his black Jeep Cherokee after closing out the bar. He absolutely has no business driving right now, so this should be fun. Drunkards like him are so much quicker to anger. I run a Clorox wipe across my steering wheel, remove the nacho cheese from my fingers, then put on my black nitrile gloves in preparation for the fun we're about to have.

Once he finally pulls off, I do as well, rounding the corner to follow him with my lights off, allowing the darkness to conceal my presence. As we reach a nice stretch of back road on his way back home, that's when it's time to reveal myself. I flip on my high beams and tailgate the fuck out of him.

Then I fall back to give him a false sense of security before picking up the pace and riding his bumper again.

I chuckle to myself when he finally slams on the brakes and hops out of the car, just like they always do. Abusers and their hot temperaments are so predictable.

As he aggressively ambles toward my car yelling and swearing, I turn off my headlights. Under the impression that he's won this battle, he returns to his car. Silly rabbit. So, I flip my high beams back on and smile, even though I know he can't see me.

He angrily stumbles up to my truck's driver's side and pounds on my tinted window, still fussing obscenities.

As I slowly roll down my window and we make eye contact, he yells, "What the fuck is-" Then he recognizes me. But it's fine because he won't be here much longer to tell anyone. "Hey, I know you..."

"No, you don't."

"Yes I do! Why are you following me!? You're the one who was-"

Before he can finish that accusatory sentence, I pull the trigger, pumping 50,000 volts of electricity into his slender midsection. He stares painfully into my eyes as he grunts, convulses, then hits the ground.

In the still of the night, I hop out of my truck and shock him again before violently yanking the Taser barbs from this predator's chest. Then I generously allow him to enjoy the sweet smell of my chloroform-doused rag before struggling to load him onto the cargo bed.

Fucking Tasers. I should have just used the stun gun. I brush myself off and stamp my feet a few times before hopping into his running car and driving it forward about 150 feet. We need to get away from the Taser confetti that explodes everywhere every time the weapon is fired. Fuck. Those damn pieces will surely identify my weapon, so I do my best to kick what confetti I can to the side of the road so it won't accidentally get tracked down to this idiot's vehicle by passing cars.

If the weathermen get it right, the rain later this morning should wash it right down the storm drain ahead.

With my new friend in the back, I should be polite. "Hey buddy, what kind of music would you like to listen to?"

...

I flip through the stations until I land on the perfect song. "Oh, you like Alanis Morissette too?"

...

"Yeah, she's pretty hot. Great voice too."

We listen to Ironic, a song that is quite fitting for this situation. Joe here hurt people, so I'll hurt him... slowly. We rock out all the way back to my place while I consider what to do with him and which piece of him I would like to share with Pittsburgh.

A smile slowly spreads across my face as I come up with a most brilliant idea - I think he should remove it himself this time.

20

Dr. Berardi slowly opened the flower box and removed the clear plastic bag containing the limb. Laying it gently on the tray, she carefully opened it to reveal a left hand and forearm, which she assessed from all angles before setting it down on the tray. She gathered the box and the plastic, manipulating it as little as possible to not potentially damage or lose evidence.

Still completely confused by this entire situation, Claudia stopped by to see Alessandra personally to verify that it was, in fact, her biological father and learn more about what happened. She entered the room slowly and apprehensively.

Without even looking up, "Good afternoon, detective."

"How do you always know it's me?"

Alessandra simply offered a sarcastic chuckle in response, then followed with, "I assume you're here about the arm."

"It was a whole arm this time? Not just a hand?"

"Yes. Sawed off just above the elbow. We haven't been able to determine if the same equipment was used to remove the limb as the others yet, though this one appears less structured and more rushed," she noted, pointing out the jaggedness of the decomposing flesh. "The only difference is he was not deceased nearly as long because there is significantly more blood at the site, which means it hadn't completely coagulated before the limb was sliced through."

Claudia had feelings she couldn't quite identify as she looked down at her father's arm on the cold metal tray. She couldn't help but wonder where the rest of him was. There was no evidence that would lead them to the location of the other victims' bodies, so how were they supposed to find *his*? It was his brushed platinum wedding band on a discolored ring finger shining brightly under the harsh LED spotlight that made Claudia wonder what type of closure her stepmother would ever have if they couldn't find his body.

"His wife was able to make a positive ID based on the wedding ring and the tattoo beneath it, but we'll still confirm it with the fingerprints - which is also very strange because the previous victims' fingerprints were destroyed. We had to use DNA to make the match. In this situation, it was almost like the killer *wanted* us to know who this man was and be able to readily identify him."

Receiving no verbal response from Claudia, Alessandra continued, "I uh… noticed his wife seemed very fond of you. May I ask how you are acquainted with his family?"

Claudia continued to stare down at the limb without a response, her mind very clearly elsewhere.

"Hmmm, Okay," she replied, taking her silence as a no. "So I have the box and the bag all ready for the crime lab to see if they can collect any additional evidence or prints."

"Thank you," Claudia nodded and turned to leave.

As she was halfway to the exit, Alessandra announced, "It's the fragrance you wear."

"Pardon me?" Claudia inquired curiously.

"It's very... *distinct*. That's also how I know you're fucking my husband. I wasn't sure if was you or your partner, but now that you're here alone, it's you. I can smell your cheap toilet water on him."

Claudia deeply inhaled erratically, closed her eyes, and let out a long sigh as she opened them to see Alessandra coming from around the table.

"Did he tell you we're having another baby?"

Still breathing heavily, Claudia stared this woman down with daggers in her eyes. Her father had just been murdered. Now was *not* the time to start with her.

"Have you *nothing* to say for yourself?" Alessandra asked, approaching her. "Stay out of my fucking marriage and keep your hands off my fucking husband, *trash*. Or I will absolutely report you for Conduct Unbecoming... let your *boss* know what you've been doing."

Claudia chuckled, "I see why West liked you... initially," she said with a darker but easy tone to her voice.

"West?" she repeated, shocked that another woman had nicknamed her husband.

"You're actually cute when you're feisty," Claudia continued as smooth as melted butter, "I think a more viable solution to this issue is maybe you keep spreading your legs for whoever *you're* fucking. Why are you even worried about what *we're* doing if *you're* doing the same thing with another man?"

Her eyes widened. "Excuse me?" she asked incredulously. She started to back away from Claudia because she'd never heard her sound so intense. She began to think maybe she'd gone a little too far with the name-calling. After all, Claudia *did* carry a gun.

"Do you even *know* whose baby it is?" she asked, slowly and slyly approaching the good doctor. "Oh yeah... he told *me* you went and got knocked up. What he didn't tell *you* is that he had a vasectomy a few months ago."

Alessandra slowly exhaled as she averted her eyes while backing away from Claudia, who was still slinking toward her like a poisonous snake. "That's a lie!" she whispered desperately, praying that it wasn't true.

"I have no reason to lie to you," she said, continuing her stealthy approach. "You're carrying another man's baby and your husband *knows* it. So if *I'm* the trash, you're the whole damn dumpster."

While Claudia may have been a solid six inches shorter than Alessandra, she was much stronger, more athletic, and more physically intimidating than the would-be supermodel. Weston's beautiful monster was all bark, no bite.

She kept approaching as Alessandra continued retreating until the back of her knees hit the edge of the folding chair situated against the wall, and she fell backward onto it. Now seated, looking up at her, tears began to well in her vulnerable brown eyes while Claudia continued her unrelenting tirade.

"So go ahead and file whatever complaint you feel is necessary." She squatted in front of the Dr. to look her square on. "Hell, I'll tell the captain my*self*. But know this... I am *quite* fond of West, and I will continue fucking him as often as I see fit. And if he *does* decide to ever fuck *you* again, rest assured, he'll be thinking about *me*." She retrieved a tissue from the box on the table beside her, handed it to the mommy-to-be, got up, and walked away.

As Claudia reached the door, she turned back around, "Oh uhh," she said softly, "I don't suppose you had a cupcake sent to my office the other day?"

She looked at her as a single tear rolled down her cheek, "Why would I buy you baked goods? You already have my husband. Isn't that enough?"

Claudia's eyes widened and she silently turned to exit the room through the stainless steel double doors.

*****

Claudia walked through the squad room toward her desk and could feel eyes on her after the events that took place at the crime scene earlier.

"So, was it his?" Lainey asked softly.

"I recognized the ring, so it's likely. What's even more fucked up is the fact that it was his left hand. He was left-handed," she whispered back. "So even if he did live through that ordeal, he would never operate again. His livelihood would have been ruined."

The captain briskly exited his office and loudly announced, "This is not good. It wasn't good before, but it's definitely worse now. This man was a highly decorated, renowned surgeon. Please tell me we have *some*thing."

No one responded, until a detective finally spoke up, "We don't have a domestic call for this address which was the only similarity among the others - abusive father, one child."

"So then how does he connect? There has to be a connection somehow."

"I think it's me. I think I'm the common denominator," Claudia hesitantly expressed to the team.

Higgins looked at her skeptically so she continued, "I had some part in every one of those calls."

"Except there was no call for the Walker family."

"Dr. Walker was my biological father – I'm his only living child."

The detectives showed looks of visible confusion, so Claudia continued, "My mother was Mexican; I have *her* last name."

"I hate to ask this, but was he ever abusive?"

"He wasn't in my life growing up, but I've never gotten controlling or aggressive vibes from him during the time he was."

"Okay, hear me out," Lainey interjected. "Was this even the same person? All of the other body parts were left in very public places. Then this one was conveniently hand-delivered to his wife's doorstep? So it's either our same guy who's escalating and getting sloppy, or it's a copycat. It's been on the news, so it's not out of the realm of possibilities."

"I stopped by the M.E.'s office, and she did mark some key differences between this one and the previous victims. She mentioned that they'd all been deceased at least six hours before the removal of the limbs, but Dr. Walker's arm was removed sooner. She also noted that the fingerprints were still intact, whereas the others weren't."

"I spoke to his colleagues and the Chief of Surgery. Dr. Walker didn't appear to have any beef with anyone that they knew of there. Everyone seemed to love him," Lainey added. "They're sending over his email history and we have phone records coming to see if maybe there were any disgruntled patients or any similarities with the others' records. We're also expecting Micah's Florals delivery records from the past three months to see if maybe someone who received a delivery could've used that box. He said his floral shop didn't have any deliveries scheduled for the Walker's address."

"Long shot, but I'll take it. What about the doorbell cam on the house?" Higgins inquired.

"Mrs. Walker pulled up the app so I could take a look," Lockhart replied. "There were no motion events last night."

"How the hell is that possible? Someone obviously left the package *on* the porch."

"Yes, but if the person snuck along the front of the house here," he explained, pointing at the area in the photo taped to the whiteboard, "dropped it quickly enough and retreated, the doorbell cam wouldn't pick it up. I once had a FedEx delivery driver walk up the sidewalk, up my three stairs, take a twenty-pound package and my doorbell didn't pick any of it up."

"Then why the hell do we have these damn cameras?" Higgins asked in the calmest possible tone he could muster, which really wasn't that calm. "Where's the car? Do we have his last known location?"

"His wife said he drove himself to the airport," Burgess replied. "GPS puts his car in the garage, but obviously he never made it onto the plane. The only camera angles we have are located in the elevator stairwell and at the midpoint of each floor. We see his car enter, but no footage of *him* at any of the egress points. So he was taken straight from the garage."

"What about Isaiah?" Claudia whispered to Lainey.

"What about him?"

"I mean, think about it. He was at all the crime scenes that I was at, but he claims he didn't commit any of the murders. Then he asked me to help him exonerate his father, I said no, and then mysteriously *my* biological father is killed?"

"I want doorbell footage from every neighbor in that cul-de-sac," Higgins shouted. "Our unsub *had* to have gotten out of that neighborhood somehow. So maybe one of the other cameras picked up a person, or a car... something." The captain ran his hand through his thick gray hair in exasperation. "We have literally got *nothing* here. This unsub is eight steps ahead of us and we need to close that distance. *Now!*"

21

Claudia's emotions were like a roller coaster on an unstable rusty track. One minute, her mood was smooth and steady. Then the next, it was crashing down onto everyone around her. The stress of being tasked with locating a serial killer who was so far ahead of them, combined with being the object of some psycho's obsession, had her constantly on edge. Add to that the fact that he was now harming people close to her had Claudia teetering on the precipice of a breakdown.

Many moments she felt indifferent to the fact that her biological father had passed away. Then others, she had feelings but she didn't know what they were or how to even describe them. Claudia sat calmly but Dr. Pearce could see that she was anything but as she bit and picked at her cuticles.

"It's not really sadness... It's more like, damn. Someone just brutally murdered him."

"I understand. Are you still on the case?"

"I am. The captain considered taking me off, but no one even knew we were related. We weren't close. I feel like I can maintain my objectivity in this situation and fortunately, he agreed."

Claudia stood up and walked over to the window to observe the pedestrians below. "I think it's more concern. Where is he? Is he still watching me? I'm just... anxious."

"So tell me about the feeling you're having that you're still being watched."

Claudia turned back toward Dr. Pearce. "I thought the feeling would dissipate once we found out that it was my brother but-"

"Wait, I'm so sorry to interrupt, but can I stop you there? Brother?"

Realizing amid all the chaos, Claudia completely neglected to mention him to Dr. Pearce. "Yeah, it's been a pretty interesting week. We found out about Isaiah when we apprehended him outside of the station. He said he had been following me to work up the courage to ask for help to exonerate his father... Miles."

Dr. Pearce was rarely at a loss for words but her face said them all, even though that was not her intention. "Wow... Okay. Can we take a few seconds to process this? I feel like I definitely need a second."

"Who are *you* tellin'?! I've had *many* seconds and I *still* don't think I've processed it all."

"I guess I'm just curious as to why he would think you'd want to help him with this painful undertaking."

"Oh, there's *so* much to be curious about here. Like why wouldn't my parents tell me that I even had a brother? Why did I have to find out like this... decades later?"

Dr. Pearce paused to think of a diplomatic way to word her thoughts. "You witnessed a man take your mother's life, which already hurt and traumatized you, would attempting to create a relationship with his son be the healthiest option for you at that point?" She paused. "That is the question I would have posed to your parents back then. Maybe the therapist back then posed a similar question?"

Claudia sat quietly taking in what she just heard.

"Also, not knowing what his adoptive parents were going to do with the information about Miles. Would they tell Isaiah and allow visitation with his father, thus risking access to you if you're in Isaiah's life?" Dr. Pearce continued, "I don't know if they made the right decision, but they made the decision that was right for them at that moment for your well-being and safety."

Claudia nodded, still considering that explanation, even though there was nothing she could do about it at this point.

"I haven't seen him around since, but I still can't shake that feeling," Claudia expressed, making her way back over to the window.

Dr. Pearce walked to her desk and opened the drawer to retrieve her prescription pad. "I'll write you a script to take when you're feeling like your anxiety is unmanageable. Something low dosage, only if you want to. But at least you'll have it. Don't drink alcohol when you take this, though."

Claudia agreed as she pulled her vibrating phone from her back pocket and read the message. "Oh shit! I'm sorry to cut this short, but I gotta run. Thanks for this," she said, shoving the prescription into her jacket pocket as she darted out of the office toward her vehicle.

*****

Claudia pulled up to the spot where Tenth St. meets Exchange Way. Officers had just finished roping it off, but that didn't stop the moving pedestrians from turning into static onlookers.

This was one of the many Pittsburgh alleyways situated between the back doors of businesses for a few blocks. As far as the eye could see down the alley, there were dumpsters for each business and fire escapes side-by-side that provided a secondary egress for residents living in the apartments above the shops. Owners and managers were coming out in droves wanting to know what was going on behind their places of business, while many residents hung out on their fire escapes above, watching the scene unfold below.

As Claudia made her way down the alley toward the captain, she noticed that the only camera possibly pointing in this direction would be the one from the Westin Hotel directly across the street.

Being sandwiched between two tall structures, unless the wind blew in a certain direction, there was very little airflow, making the garbage truck's horrific odor even more aggressive.

Claudia barely recognized Alessandra who was wearing white coveralls with gloves up her forearms and a face mask while going through a black garbage bag. She couldn't help but think to herself, *at least she won't be able to smell me now.* They exchanged glances, but Alessandra quickly diverted her attention back to her task.

The cigarette smoke from one of the sanitation workers was a welcome change from the putrid odor emanating from the back of the nearby truck.

As Claudia peeked inside the back, she listened as one of the workers explained what happened to Lainey and two other officers.

"So the bag was on top of the dumpster, but we gotta open the lids before we can hitch it up to the back of the truck to empty it," the worker said, using his entire body to tell the story. "It didn't look full so I didn't think it'd be heavy, but it was, so it kinda hit the ground first before I flung it into the hopper. Then I hooked up the dumpster and emptied it. Did that a couple a more times, then we came to another bag! It was heavy too, so when that one hit the ground, I opened it cuz sometimes people fill contractor bags wit' all kindsa shit we ain't allowed to take. I know for *damn* sure we ain't allowed to take *dead* people, man! I need a new job! But not theirs," he said, referencing the two investigators who were knee-deep in the hopper, rummaging through it to locate the recently discarded body parts.

"Then what happened?"

"I heard him scream," the second worker said in less vivid detail. "So I hopped out to see what happened. I thought it was fake, but the smell was worse than the truck. I looked down the alley and saw that there was one more bag on top of the dumpster, so that's when we called our dispatch to report it, then they called yinz guys," he said, then took another drag of his cigarette.

Lainey handed them both her card in case they remembered anything else, then she and Claudia made their way back down to where the medical examiner was working.

"You realize where we're at, right?" Lainey asked.

When Claudia didn't respond, Lainey continued, "We're less than a block from Micah's Florals. The back of his store is right down there. Whoever left these bags easily could have grabbed a box from back there... No cameras, though."

"Just the one across the street at the Westin, but I don't know which direction it faces because it's inside the black housing case."

"Detectives," Alessandra greeted as they approached. "Dr. Walker was our only African-American victim so far. I would say that these three bags contain his remains. Of course, I will verify this with prints and DNA, but the hand in this bag looks the same as the other... except it's missing his watch. I overheard Mrs. Walker say that he always wore the silver engraved Tag Heuer watch that she gave him."

"Thank you," Lainey said as Alessandra walked toward her van.

"We should check the local pawn shops. They definitely have cameras; maybe we can get a hit," Claudia suggested.

"Absolutely. But hey, look at this." Lainey pointed out the three small tufts of blankets and other materials near some of the dumpsters. "Someone's been living, or at least sleeping here." They began to scan the spectators in hopes that the owners of those spots were nearby waiting for everyone to clear out so they could reclaim their territory.

As soon as Claudia made eye contact with the disheveled individual, he immediately averted his eyes and began to hobble away from the scene with his shopping cart.

Claudia grabbed Lainey's attention and they caught up to him relatively quickly.

"What's the hurry there, sir?" Lainey asked as Claudia walked around to the front of his cart to prevent him from going any further.

"Oh... I- uh..." the man faltered as he fearfully looked back and forth between the two detectives and behind them at the other police officers.

"I'm Detective Crane. This is Detective Martinez. What's your name?"

The man replied with only heavy breathing and nervous glances before quietly uttering, "John."

"Got a last name, John?"

"Doe," he blurted out nervously.

Lainey and Claudia exchanged looks, "Okay, Mr. *Doe*. "Were you around here last night?"

"Uh-uh... No," he said too quickly to be the truth. "No, I was uhh..."

Claudia sensed that he was lying, so she pressed a little more forcefully, "Tell us what you saw last night."

"Nothing! I swear!" the terrified man responded immediately before she could even finish the question.

Dirt and overgrown gray facial hair covered his worn face, but his clear gray eyes were visible and wide with panic.

"Look, obviously we know you didn't do this. We just want to find out if you or any of your friends saw anything at all that could help us," Lainey said calmly.

He immediately shook his head no, as Claudia stepped away, summoned by Tanner.

"Okay, sir. Thank you," Lainey sighed.

As she began to walk away, he grabbed her forearm and whispered, "Wait!" His eyes were so full of fear, but he looked like he desperately wanted to tell her something.

He leaned in closer to her just as Tanner and Claudia were approaching them. Lainey ignored the smell of the man and leaned in for whatever he was about to reveal, but instead, he stopped, glancing fearfully among the three of them. "Um... Do you... have a dollar to spare?"

A disappointed Lainey replied, "Sure," as she handed him a five from her pocket. He thanked her and then quickly hobbled away but still looked back at them periodically.

"That man was terrified. I know he saw something," Lainey said to her two colleagues. "I'm gonna come back tomorrow when there are fewer people and no police. See if he'll talk to me then."

Claudia awakened peacefully for the first time in a while with no alarm clock or night terrors ripping her forcefully from a sound night's sleep. It was refreshing, though ironic, considering her biological father had just been murdered. She was undoubtedly the target of some psychopath's ire, yet last night was the most calmly she'd slept in months. She had been doing the visualization exercises Dr. Pearce gave her, but she didn't think they had been helping. Maybe they finally were?

She turned on the television to listen to the news while getting ready for work, only to see her father's headshot on the screen. He was clean-cut with a smooth dark complexion accentuated by the salt and pepper throughout his facial hair. Claudia was instantly annoyed by the warm smile that made him look like he was the salt of the fucking earth.

"... *And today The University of Pittsburgh Medical Center family mourns the loss of one of their own. Dr. Darrell Claude Walker was a prominent fertility specialist in the Reproductive and Endocrinology department at Magee Women's Hospital in Oakland. We have been told that his* death is part of an ongoing investigation in which police have very few leads. They are asking that anyone who could have-"

"*No* leads is more like it," Claudia muttered as she turned off the television. Amazing how her surgeon father received prime-time news coverage, but the deaths of the three men prior were barely a blip on anyone's radar – just a story here and there. Not that she had much sympathy for them, considering they'd been abusing their families. But it's just amazing what money and status could get you.

*****

"I'm pulling up the hotel footage now, eyes up!" Lainey shouted as everyone gathered around the flat screen monitor in the squad room. "The bags could only have been left one of the past six nights before that week's garbage pick-up."

While the camera angle only barely caught the first dumpster on the left, there was a garbage bag there, so they would at least be able to see who left it. Hopefully, that was their unsub. The room fell silent and thick with tension as Lainey quickly jumped through each night looking for bags to appear until she finally made it to the last night before pick-up.

"Well, this has to be it," she said, slowly forwarding through the footage.

"Look at that!" Detective Lockhart shouted as they all watched the man with the shopping cart hobble over to interact with the stranger out of camera range. All that was visible were the suspect's long concealed arms and black-gloved hands as the bags were loaded on top of what items were already in his cart. They watched as the homeless man accepted money from the hidden stranger, then struggled to push the cart down to the first dumpster on the left, where he then fought to unload the first bag. After that, he was no longer in camera range.

"Well, no wonder he didn't wanna talk and seemed scared to death," Lockhart announced. "*He* left the damn bags! He likely talked to our killer and we let him walk away... with *your* money, no less," he glared at Lainey.

"Find him!" Captain Higgins yelled. "I want him here! *Today!*"

*****

"What if he wanted to tell us that one of the officers paid him? What if he recognized someone on the scene?" Lainey asked as they drove back to the alley to find the witness.

"Why would one of our officers want to murder my father? Or stalk *me* for that matter?"

"Well, that's what I'm having a little trouble putting together. But he was gonna tell me *something* yesterday like, I *know* it." She paused to reflect. "The way he grabbed me... it was chilling. Then you and Tanner came over and he chickened out."

"Are you saying you think it was Tanner who recognized?"

"I'm not saying it was. But I'm not saying it wasn't. You don't think it's suspicious that he *insisted* on taking you home that night you blacked out? He lied about knowing where you lived."

As much as Claudia didn't want to keep secrets from her partner, the reality was her personal business was her own. But she decided to come clean anyway.

"Lainey. Tanner and I kinda hooked up... A little bit."

"What!?" she screeched.

"That's how he knew where I lived. I don't often invite people over, but I figured, he's the police. I'm the police. It's fine. Definitely starting to re-think that now," she mumbled.

"So all that time when I was trying to get you to talk to him, you were already doing way more than *talking*?"

"I'm only telling you so you're not using *just* that as a reason to cast suspicion onto him. But I honestly wouldn't be surprised if it were an inside job. My head's been on a swivel for months now, paying attention to everything and everyone, but no one is standing out. So I don't know where to go with that."

As the detectives pulled up on Tenth St., Lainey leaned into Claudia, "I only have one final question to ask..." Then she smirked and stared at Claudia like she already knew the question.

"I mean... I *guess* it was okay? For some reason, I don't quite remember *that* much about it."

"What does that even mean!? You think he drugged you *before* your birthday?"

"I thought I told you the tox screen came back clean. So no, he didn't drug me on *or* before my birthday. But we'd been drinking, so I'm guessing that's why the slight sexual memory lapse?"

"Well, any man who can get you out of those long sleeve shirts is still okay in my book, memorable sex or not! How are you not sweltering right now?"

"It's light. I'm cozy," Claudia chuckled, adjusting her sleeves.

They strolled down the alley searching for their witness, hoping he hadn't gotten scared off and switched locations in the last twenty-four hours.

"There!" Lainey pointed down the alley where only the edge of a shopping cart was visible behind the giant green dumpster.

They approached to find him lying in a fetal position, covered in a tattered plaid blanket and a few newspapers.

Lainey kneeled and gently shook his body to awaken him, but he didn't rouse.

"Sir?" she said, trying again but still getting no response. She looked up at Claudia, then felt the side of his neck for the pulse that was nonexistent.

"You gonna tell me this is not a *fucking* inside job?!" Lainey shouted. "Police were *all* over the scene yesterday. We *talked* to him. We *all* saw him on video. Now he's *dead*!? The only link to our killer and he's dead," she ranted as she stormed away to make the call.

"Dispatch, this is Detective Crane. We have a 10-54 in Exchange Way. And I want the medical examiner!"

Claudia looked up at the surrounding fire escapes to see if anyone was watching, but they appeared to be alone.

Lainey returned huffing, "That man did *not* die of natural causes."

*****

Weston entered his home, arms full of grocery bags that he sat down at the door. Through the open floor concept, he noticed Alessandra seated at the head of the dining room table. Her demeanor was calm, her face like stone, her gaze like daggers boring through his chest. If looks could kill, he would most certainly be a dead man. But that was nothing new. She averted her piercing brown eyes from him down to the laptop, quietly watching whatever was on the screen.

"Where are the boys?" Weston asked as he loaded the grocery bags onto the island. "Those cookies they like are back in stores," he chuckled to himself, receiving no response from his wife.

Once Weston stopped talking and rustling the bags long enough, he was able to hear the low audio playing on Alessandra's computer. He immediately recognized the passionate sounds of sex. He stood speechless, staring at his wife mildly intrigued, "Are you watching *porn*!?"

"Your detective outright *told* me she was going to continue fucking you." Alessandra stood up and strode toward her husband. "But I didn't expect her to send it to me in a fucking *video*!" she yelled.

"Wait, *what*?" Weston still stood shocked unable to believe that Claudia would even *say* those things, let alone send his wife a video of them having sex.

"Okay, yes. She and I have been having an affair. I'm sorry, but-"

"*Sorry*?" She forcefully interrupted. "You're only sorry because you got *caught*!"

"Hey! Where's *your* apology? *You're* caught too. You know damn well that's not my baby!"

Alessandra lowered her head to the left and didn't respond. "Yeah... She told me about your vasectomy, you lying bastard!" she screamed as she grabbed the nearby bottle of wine and chucked it at his head. He slid to the right dodging the glass bottle which shattered against the edge of the marble counter behind him. "Why am I hearing about a vasectomy, that *we* never discussed, from your fucking *mistress*!?"

"I was gonna tell you. But either way, you're not innocent in *any* of this!" he roared.

"Why?" Alessandra quietly asked, on the verge of tears. "Why *her*? You told her you *love* her."

"Ohh come off it, Alli! Stop with the sad puppy dog eyes. You're more in love with your designer possessions and your money than you've ever been with me!" he yelled back angrily. "You just hop on top of me for the ride and that's it. Where's the affection? The sensitivity? Where's the intimacy? I get none of that! Gahh! You won't even suck my dick!"

"So you cheated on me over a blowjob?"

"It's like you're not even listening... And do you even *hear* yourself!? Why did *you* cheat, Alessandra?" he asked, getting in her face.

"Because you're never *home*! I'm *lonely*!" she shouted without backing down. "I guess now I know why." Her hand met the side of his face with a loud smack just before she collected her red Prada bag and headed toward the door.

"Nice. That's *really* fucking nice!"

Without looking back, she flipped him off and stormed out of their home.

Weston leaned back against the island, rubbing his red cheek, listening as his wife pulled off in what sounded like her Mercedes Sportster. He looked at the floor, watching as the expanding puddle of wine slowly crept toward his feet. Instead of immediately cleaning it up, he sat at Alessandra's laptop and watched the video of Claudia bent over the railing of her deck. His body rhythmically crashed into her thick bottom, one hand full of her curly hair and the other arm around her waist, helping to drive himself deeper inside. Their eager but passionate love cries echoed softly through the empty room.

Though enraged at this situation that could potentially ruin both of their careers if leaked, arousal still managed to set in as he scrolled through the video, reflecting upon how glorious the detective felt tightly wrapped around him. But he knew it had to go, so Weston deleted it from the desktop, then permanently from the recycle bin. He opened his wife's email and did the same, then checked the sent folder to see if his wife had forwarded it to anyone, which it didn't appear as though she had. He angrily pulled out his cell phone to FaceTime Claudia.

"Well you're a site for sore eyes, handsome... Wait, are you calling me from your house?" She could see the anger in his face, "What's wrong?"

"Claudia, what the *fuck* did you do!?"

"What are you talking about?" she asked confused.

"You sent my wife a video of us having *sex*... on your *deck*? There's a camera out there?"

"I mean, yeah... I have cameras all over the place now, I- I didn't realize... Weston I promise, I wouldn't send her a video!"

"Why would I believe that? You're the one who told her about our affair! She said you even told her about my vasectomy," he angrily hissed.

"No! No! *She* confronted *me*. She knew we were sleeping together. Said she could smell me on *your* clothes. Everything after that is... I don't know, but I- it wasn't intentional..."

"So I told you I wasn't leaving her yet and you go and do *this* shit, to what? Expedite the process? Claudia, the email came from *your* address!"

"No! No, no, no, that's impossible!"

"Who else would do this? Tell me! Who? *Who!?*" he screamed.

"I don't *know!*" she cried. "Maybe the same person who broke into my house and killed my fish? The same person who murdered my father and all those other men? The same person who's been watching me?" Claudia broke down into frustrated tears.

Weston took a beat to consider everything she said, "I don't know... it all just seems a little..."

After a few erratic breaths, Claudia delivered an icy gaze into the phone, "You know what, I don't need this shit right now. Fuck you *and* your slut wife."

With that, the phone went black. Weston tried three times to call her back, but she declined his calls.

23

Her cell phone rang almost non-stop for the duration of Claudia's commute to work. As hell-bent as Weston was on reaching her, she was just as determined to get to the station and then get out into the field so he wouldn't be able to ambush her there. She was pissed that his whore of a wife had a pornographic video of them and in her angered state, heaven only knew what she'd do with it. But she was even more infuriated that Weston would accuse *her* of sending it. That video would have noticeably incriminated her, so that was the absolute last thing Claudia would want out in the world. As she thought back to all the filthy things she said during their love session, it made her even queasier and she prayed that Weston had the good sense to permanently delete the video.

She was awake that entire night wondering who could've gained access to not only the video feed but also her personal email. Or maybe it was made to *look* like it came from her. Either way, none of it was okay.

Claudia spent much of the night going through all of the "motion event notifications" from her security cameras, with nothing to show other than animals triggering it. But she was well aware that if someone *were* savvy enough to have hacked into the system to obtain that video of them, or if they *were* ever on the premises, of course they would have deleted that particular event notification. None of it sat well with Claudia because what was the point of having the cameras then?

As Claudia was about to enter the squad room, Lainey ran over to catch her before she made it through the double doors.

"Hey! Morning!" she panted, slightly out of breath. "How are you? You okay?"

Claudia nodded unconvincingly.

"Well, before you go in there, I wanted to grab you to give you a heads up. Higgins was losing his entire shit so I *kinda* mentioned your theory about Isaiah. Just to see what he thought."

"Oh boy, what'd he say?" she asked, sipping her iced coffee.

"He wanted Isaiah brought back in for questioning. Detective Torrey went to pick him up about an hour ago."

"Well, he's not gonna be happy about that," Claudia replied as they walked toward their desks.

"Very true," Lainey agreed. "Sooo, Starbucks today? No Steamy Bean with free pastries from your li'l boy crush?"

Claudia shot her a look. "No," she said, placing her items on the desk and opening her laptop.

"Hey, there he is. Let's go." Lainey grabbed her folder, pen, and pad, then headed to the interrogation room.

From across the room, Claudia watched Isaiah, with that familiar stroll, follow Torrey through the squad room and down the hall until he was out of sight. She then went to join the others in the observation room.

"So, thank you for voluntarily coming back in," the detective said to Isaiah.

He simply rolled his eyes as he was escorted into the interrogation room once again. Anxiously pacing the room, he wondered how many people were watching him through the two-way mirror. He also couldn't help but speculate if this was how his father felt when the police railroaded him into a conviction. Isaiah knew he'd done nothing wrong and was having trouble concealing his irritation with this entire situation.

"Haven't seen you at any more of our crime scenes, Mr. Mills," Lainey said casually as she entered the room.

"Exactly. You have not. So why am I here?" Isaiah inquired as they both sat down.

"Oh, you haven't spoken to Detective Martinez at all?"

"Not since I asked her to help my father and she rudely declined," he said, squirming in the hard metal seat.

"Hmmm, okay, we're investigating something and we just need to know where you were last week."

"The whole week? Care to narrow that down at all, detective?"

"Mmmm, no." Lainey shook her head and clicked her pen, ready to start writing on the white notepad in front of her.

With a sigh, Isaiah removed his cell phone from his pocket and opened his calendar app. "Well from the sixth to the eleventh, I was in Knoxville for a work conference."

"Nice. My family's from down there – I still go home for the holidays. Where did you stay?"

"The Tennessean."

"Wow, that's a pretty extravagant hotel. Your company paid for that? Who do you work for?"

"QX Communications... In sales. They provide a stipend for hotel stays, but I elected to pay the difference and stay somewhere much nicer."

"Of course you did. When did you get back?"

"My fiancée picked me up at around 10:45 the night of the eleventh."

"And the rest of the week?"

"Ummm, just work. I met some friends at Shorty's that Friday night, and then that weekend, my fiancée and I did a bunch of wedding stuff. Cake tasting and linens and crap."

Lainey continued writing.

"You never did say what you were investigating."

"Mr. Mills, I'm sure you've seen the news. Someone murdered a very prominent physician."

"And you think *I* could possibly do something like that?"

"Between us," Lainey leaned in, "I don't think you did, but considering that he was Detective Martinez's biological father, some of the boys in the back just kinda thought that *maybe*... you didn't take too kindly to having your request for help be... 'rudely declined.' *Your* words."

"What?!"

"Yeah. She didn't help your father, so you-"

"*Killed* hers!?" Isaiah interrupted. "That's ludicrous! What kind of logic is that?"

"You know, you'd be shocked how often there is zero logic involved when people wanna just kill other people," she replied blithely. "Okay," she said, getting up from the cold metal table. "We'll verify this and if it all checks out, you won't hear from us again."

"Good," Isaiah muttered under his breath.

"After you," she gestured, following him out of the interrogation room.

Claudia exited the observation room and followed Isaiah out to the elevators.

"Isaiah."

"What do you want? You told me to stay away from you - I have. Now they think I killed your dad?" he whispered furiously.

"Look, we're just doing our jobs, covering our bases. We don't have that many leads."

"Okay, well you still don't because *I* am not one of them! Just like you guys to want to pin this shit on a Black man."

"Seriously!? In case you've forgotten," Claudia dramatically swiped her finger across her cheek to remind him of her *own* brown skin. "The victim was Black. Half the officers in there are Black, so this isn't about your skin color."

He glanced over her shoulder through the glass wall, on some level, just to verify what she was saying. He had never even noticed. Growing up in such an affluent area with very few people of color, he was used to getting profiled from a very young age, even though he was never doing anything wrong. Trauma like that tends to stay with a person.

"So, have you changed your mind about helping Miles? Because otherwise, why are you here talking to me?"

"To tell you that after you left the first time, I *did* pull up the case files. He did it, Isaiah."

"No, he *didn't*!" He shouted, slamming his hand against the closed elevator door.

"You weren't *there*. Isaiah, our mother had post-mortem bruising on the front of each shoulder."

"What's that even mean?"

"It means that someone forcefully hit the front of both of her shoulders," Claudia explained as she demonstrated using the heels of her hands to push Isaiah backward at his shoulders. "It's how she went backward down the fifteen steps. We were the only three in the house. I was six. No one else was tall enough *or* strong enough to do that, which was pretty much why he was convicted. How do you deny that?"

"I don't know. But I'm telling you, he couldn't have done it." The elevator opened and Isaiah stepped in, "I have to believe that," he sighed. "I really wish you would just visit him... look him in the eyes, please," Isaiah pleaded with her as the door shut.

Annoyed, Claudia stormed back into the squad room, grabbed her keys and cell phone, left a note for Lainey, then headed out. She needed air.

*****

Claudia strolled through the bustling streets of Downtown Pittsburgh, visiting each of the five pawn shops in search of her father's Tag Heuer watch. She presented herself as a regular customer hoping to locate the watch before presenting herself as law enforcement. Once a badge comes out, defenses rise. She wasn't in the mood to work against them that day, and really just wanted to lay eyes on the watch first, then do what she needed to do to obtain the video footage if she found it. Unfortunately, none of it was necessary, as there were no timepieces matching that description to be found in any of the shops. Of course, there was no guarantee that the person took it to a shop in town, or even at all. But she had to start somewhere.

As Claudia made her way back to her vehicle, she pondered Isaiah's request to visit Miles. Part of her felt it was incredibly selfish and insensitive for him to ask for her help, but her other side felt like maybe she would do the same thing in his position.

She hopped into her car to head back to the station when Lainey sent a text for her to meet them on Cordell to canvas the neighborhood, talk to homeowners, and obtain any security cam footage that could possibly help with any leads.

Claudia pulled up to find Tanner had already arrived at the location. They hadn't spoken much on a personal level since her birthday gathering, so she took several deep breaths to prepare herself for the interaction.

They exchanged awkward greetings and made small talk until their colleagues arrived, even though he *wanted* to express how much he missed spending time with her, which really meant having sex with her. But he didn't feel it was appropriate, considering they were there to find out who murdered her father. Fortunately, it didn't take long for them to get back into a normal rhythm of friendly conversation.

Detective Burgess pulled up right behind Lainey who immediately hopped out of her car and started barking orders while distributing flash drives to each person. "Okay, we got one big ass cul-de-sac. This is the only way in or out, so we need to talk to these thirteen houses between Dr. Walker's home and this exit here. We're looking for footage from Tuesday night through sunrise Wednesday morning. If they don't have video doorbells or security cameras, maybe they were up and saw something. You guys split up and take that side of the street. Claudia and I will split up and take this side."

The team did their due diligence and spoke with each of the neighbors in hopes that the person who delivered the flower box was not their unsub. Your normal law-abiding citizen wouldn't necessarily think about the fact that when they walk past someone's home, they may be caught on their cameras. However, this unsub had been so meticulous that if he *were* the person delivering the item, they weren't likely to find video proof of it.

As they returned to their cars one by one, Claudia asked Lainey if she had found anything.

"Not a thing. What about you?"

"Nada."

The other detectives had the same response when they arrived. No one was looking forward to giving this information to the captain.

"I'm gonna go check in on Ms. Emma while I'm out here. Update her on everything, not that we have much."

"Do you need me to come with?" Lainey asked.

"No, I'm good. See you back at the station."

Claudia slowly made her way down the block to the large white house, deep in thought, fiddling with the keys and flash drive in her jacket pocket.

24

"Absolutely!" A frazzled mom exclaimed. "It wasn't even supposed to rain, but it's just so dreary we decided to do something indoors. We're at the Science Center if you want to meet us here," she said on the phone as her three-year-old held her hand, dragging her over to the life-size Operation game. "Right now, we're on the fourth floor learning about the human body. I'm pretty sure some of this stuff will give Connor nightmares. But whatever, he's having fun."

Connor handed his mom the plastic femur he successfully removed from the game. She was so used to being handed random things by her toddler that she just took it and kept talking on the phone before realizing she shouldn't have it.

"No, baby," she whispered to him. "Take this and put it back in the game. We can't keep it."

"Okay, we'll see you guys in about twenty minutes. He'll be so excited to see his little bestie," she said to her friend on the phone.

Connor removed a few more bones from the game then tired of it, moving on to the next exhibit, where he began to disassemble the 3-D human lungs puzzle, handing pieces of it to his mother. She was holding them in both hands, balancing the phone between her shoulder and ear, "Yeah, we parked on the far side because it's so packed in here already, which is crazy because it *just* opened. So if Ted can drop you off..."

Connor put on the headphones to listen to the lung information and began to take the puzzle pieces back from his mother as she finished her phone call. She helped him reassemble the lungs, then he took her hand and dragged her over to a booth. She peeked in and there were no children inside, so she slid the curtain aside to let him in. With her attention back on her phone scrolling through social media, she barely noticed when Connor popped back out of the booth, handed her another item, then dragged her over to the next exhibit.

When she finally realized what she was holding, she gasped and went back to peek into The Human Ear booth her son exited.

She looked back down at the bluish-reddish prosthetic ear she was holding, wondering where it was supposed to go inside the exhibit, but she couldn't find a spot for it. As she examined it closer, she was slightly disturbed by how realistic these items were looking and became more concerned about *herself* having nightmares than her son.

Just across the way, there was an exhibit in which children could wear gloves and touch real organs while getting a lesson from staff on each one.

"Excuse me, hi. My son handed this to me, but it probably belongs here with you guys," she said to the two employees in white lab coats as she set it down in front of them.

They stared slowly at each other, then back to the mother who turned to check on Connor's location.

"Wait, ma'am. Where did you get this?" he asked as he slid on a pair of gloves. "Call the manager," he whispered to his colleague.

"Just over at The Human Ear booth," she pointed behind her. "You guys don't really need to make these things look so real. These are children, you know?"

The employees continued staring with great concern unsure of how to respond, so she asked, "What's the problem?"

"So this is the Animal Anatomy Exhibit. *This* doesn't belong to us."

"So then... whose... wait, that's not real, right? *Right!?*"

When the employees exchanged glances, that's when she noticed their medical school embossed lab coats.

She looked down at her hands, then immediately ran over to Connor to disinfect him.

*****

"You have got to be kidding me right now," Lainey said. "Please tell me that our unsub did *not* leave a body part in the damn Science Center!?"

"No can do, Detective. Honestly, I'm surprised it didn't happen sooner. Makes the most sense," Tanner replied.

"How do you figure?"

"They have a whole floor devoted to anatomy and physiology for the next few months. Brought my niece here a few weeks ago 'cause she wants to be a doctor. But last week she wanted to be a firefighter, so who knows."

"There are children everywhere. I just don't get it," she replied. "The unsub's objective seems to be to punish men who abused children. So why leave body parts where the same demographic he's trying to protect could potentially find them?"

"Maybe it wasn't intended for a child to find it. Maybe staff or cleaning crew, depending upon when it was left," Tanner offered as they entered through the front doors. They joined Claudia who was speaking with the tall thin manager who looked more like he should be teaching a science class than running the center.

"Hey, just in time. We're headed upstairs to the fourth floor," Claudia said.

On the way up the long oval spiral walkway, the manager pointed out where all the cameras were located. The detectives were relatively certain that there was no way their delivery man took this route. At the entrance alone, multiple cameras were facing the doors and the check-in counter.

"Are there any other points of entry that would give access to this floor?" Lainey asked.

"Just the back stairwell. But there are no cameras on each floor. Just one at the top, one at the bottom, and on all of the elevators."

"Are they working?"

"To my knowledge, yes."

"Please have your I.T. department verify that. This unsub has been known to knock out the camera systems prior to delivery. If you do have the footage, we need that ASAP," Claudia requested.

As they arrived on the anatomy floor, it had been cleared out except for the officers who were taking a statement from the mother. Photos were being taken, but they were almost certain that of the many prints that would be lifted, none of them would belong to their perp.

The medical examiner was already on the scene packaging up the ear to take back to the lab.

"Good morning, Alessandra."

"That's Dr. Berardi to you," she tersely replied to Claudia, then directed her attention to Lainey. The detective bit her tongue and held her reply, considering the whole video incident.

"I'm headed back to the lab," Alessandra said. "I don't want to be here when you tell Higgins that the owner of this ear was likely alive when it was removed and that he possibly did it to himself based on the amount of dried blood, the cut patterns, and the hesitation marks.

"Whoa! You're saying this victim cut off his *own* ear!?"

Alessandra gave a single head nod.

"Yeah, I don't wanna be here when I tell the captain that *either*," Lainey replied, rolling her eyes while running her hands through her golden tresses.

"I'll run DNA. Hopefully, he's in the system and I can get back to you soon with a name. If not, I'll put a rush on it," she said, walking away.

"So what was that about?" Lainey asked Claudia.

"What?"

"*That's Dr. Berardi to you*," she replied, mocking Alessandra.

"I have no idea," Claudia lied.

*****

"Victim is Joseph Tate, goes by Joe or JT. He was already in the system, so it was a quick match," Lainey announced from her desk. "He's got a 2019 Jeep Cherokee registered to him."

"Great, I'll see if I can get a location on that vehicle."

"Thanks," Lainey replied. "Looks like his cell phone also went down very early morning two nights ago."

"Fits our unsub's M.O.," Higgins replied, pacing the squad room.

"Uhh, not completely," Lainey interjected. "M.E. said the ear was removed while the victim was still alive, and likely by the vic himself."

"*What?*" The captain sighed. "Okay, let's keep that information close to the vest. Do we have reports on file for any domestic calls, or was he just a random victim like Dr. Walker appeared to be?"

"Oh yeah, we were there. A few months ago before any of this even started," Burgess offered. "He has a girlfriend Nova... daughter Autumn."

"But if it's just an ear, what are the chances he could still be alive?"

"I'd wager not if it's the same unsub from Martinez's cases." Higgins turned his attention to Claudia, "I take it you were at this scene too?"

"I was actually... after the fact. Mr. Tate had been drinking and hit his daughter, causing her to fall down three steps off the landing. His girlfriend attacked him for injuring the little girl and he had the audacity to try to press charges against *her*."

"That's rich. Go see what else you can find out."

Burgess sent them the coordinates of the Jeep, which they were able to locate on the way to the victim's house.

As they pulled up to the vehicle, a tall woman with loud red hair was walking around it, then opened the driver's side door.

"Excuse me, ma'am," Lainey said, quickly jumping out of her car to stop the woman from getting in and touching anything else. "You are?"

"The owner of this SUV... well, my boyfriend is... well, my ex. I needed his car," she said with a robust southern drawl even louder than her hair.

"You're Nova Parks?"

"Yes," she replied to Claudia. "I remember you – Detective Martinez, right? You're the one who stopped me from murdering that son of a bitch." She laughed, but neither of the detectives did.

"What? What's wrong?"

"Ma'am, when was the last time you saw Joseph?

"Ohhh, no need to ma'am me! Nova, please," she requested, drawing out her vowels when she spoke. "Last time I saw JT was about four days ago, but I talked to him on Sunday."

"So, what brought you *here*?"

"Are y'all not listenin'? I told y'all I needed his car. Mine was in the shop. He was 'posed to drop the Jeep off yesterday but never came with it. I figured he was out shitfaced drunk somewhere - *again*. So I got a ride to pick mine up," she gestured to the small blue Toyota illegally parked with a friend inside. "Then I opened the app and did that cute li'l *find my car* thing. We was just gonna find *his* and take it to teach him a lesson." Nova immediately covered her mouth, "Ohhhh damn it, I shouldn't be tellin' the police that, huh?" she nervously chuckled.

Claudia peeked into the Jeep's windows but nothing looked out of place, simply abandoned, much like Adam Holsinger's car was when he disappeared.

"Joseph is missing. Look. I'm gonna be honest with you, his circumstances are very much like three previous victims who are no longer alive," Lainey said gently.

"Hmmm..." Nova replied casually. "I mean if it was up to me, I'da kill't him that night. But I didn't do this one," she immediately added. "Ya know, he wasn't always like that. He just started drinkin' more when he lost his job a spell back and never quite got it back together. He started hittin' on me, but I'll fight back. When he hit my baby girl, though? No sir, no ma'am! She ain't but big as a quick minute!"

Though she probably shouldn't have, Claudia smiled, admiring Nova's fighting spirit, even though she just admitted to wanting to kill him and planned to steal his car.

"Sooo, can I take this?"

"Sorry, but no. It's now evidence in an active investigation," Claudia replied. "May I have your set of keys? They'll be returned once everything has been processed."

Nova removed the key fob from her ring, handed it over, and quickly got into her car, hoping to get away before they processed all the crazy stuff she'd just said.

"I called in a confirmation. The forensic team is coming to impound the vehicle," Lainey said as they got back into theirs. "This just seems like a really odd place to get out and confront someone."

"I mean, it's definitely out of the way and not well-traveled, especially at night. If *I* were gonna abduct someone, I would consider this location."

25

Steaming hot water beat down on Claudia's chest, cascading down her body, where she noticed another bruise forming on her thigh. She never recalled injuring herself, yet bruises would mysteriously appear. Figuring it must be from her weight training, she shifted focus back to her original thoughts. Of course, her hot water was being wasted by simply standing in the shower using that as her think tank to figure out what the hell was going on, but she didn't care. She was drowning in thoughts, emotions, and confusion and wished they would just flow away as easily as this shower water down the drain.

Claudia's breasts began to turn red from the constant onslaught of the harsh water pressure, so she turned around so her back could take the abuse while she continued reflecting. Her ringing phone that vibrated off of the sink and onto the floor put an end to that.

She answered the call on speaker and set it back on the sink while she dried off.

"Before you can even object, I'm bringing you some love."

"That really isn't necessary, Hope."

"I don't care, I'm on my way over. Besides, once you start this journey, it must be completed. Hell, I packed a snack and filled my tank to trek out there," she chuckled.

"Fiiiine, I'll see you soon," Claudia replied in defeat, even though she appreciated the gesture.

She had planned to lie around the house in her bath towel fresh out of the shower, but now she had to actually do something with herself. Standard messy bun, t-shirt, and boxers for the win.

The upside to Hope visiting to check on her meant she would be able to replace whatever processed trash she was about to eat for dinner with something of actual nutritional value. She loved to feed people too much to arrive empty-handed. And food was her love language.

Claudia quickly spruced up the common areas, fed Joffrey, and turned on *The First 48* until her big sister arrived.

When she heard someone fiddling with the lock, Claudia ran to the door to open it. "Sorry, I changed all the locks," she said, hugging Hope.

They unloaded what looked to be dinner for the next week onto the kitchen island. "Hope, this is insane! You didn't have to do all this."

"I know, but after everything that happened with your bio dad, I know you're tired and stressed, so... food!" she said with a smile as she loaded it into the relatively empty fridge.

"Well, thank you. I really appreciate it," Claudia replied, replacing her old house key from the chain with the new one. "New key. It opens the front and the back."

Since she was closer to the trash can, Hope held her hand out, "Want me to pitch that one?"

"No, I'll hang on to it, but thanks," she replied anxiously, rubbing it between her fingers. "So what'd you bring?"

"The meal prep for the next five days has snapper, chicken, and pork chops, but I knew nothing would cheer up my CoCo like some lobster mac n cheese!" she said, pulling out a fork from the drawer. "Though I don't know how you could possibly have an appetite after watching *that*."

Claudia glanced at the TV, which displayed some rather gruesome crime scene footage. "It doesn't really bother me... the images. Just when it's kids and elderly people, that's the most unsettling for me."

Claudia took the fork and the cheesy seafood dish and set it on the coffee table, then headed back for the oversized bottle of white wine. Hope drove, so her libation limit was one glass, which left the remainder for Claudia as she filled Hope in on everything. She hadn't shared with her what happened the night of the party, or the fact that she was convinced someone had *still* been trailing her and all the horrible things they'd done to scare her. She also came clean about Weston being married, which immediately made Hope think that his wife was the one stalking her. That wasn't out of the realm of possibilities. When Hope pulled up Alessandra's social media page, her first response was, "Oh, it's definitely her! Look at her! She's gorgeous... and looks crazy as hell!"

Claudia needed that laugh. She then went on to discuss finding her father's body parts dumped like he was common trash. Hope was beside herself because she had no idea her sister was dealing with that much madness, all alone when she could've just called. She'd always been there for Claudia and some nut-job stalker wasn't going to change that.

A giant bowl of lobster mac, a whole bottle of wine, and a great many tears later, it was only 8:20 p.m. and Claudia had already fallen asleep on the couch. Hope turned off her television, covered her with a blanket, and locked the door on her way out.

*****

Just as the ivory fleece cover was being slowly moved down her smooth bare legs, Claudia jolted herself upright breathing heavily in a cold sweat. Gazing furiously around the room, it took her a minute to acclimate to her surroundings and realize she was not in her bed, but that she was alone and safe. She squeezed her eyes shut willing the bad images in her subconscious mind to leave, as she yanked out her bun to shake out her damp hair. The enormous decorative metal clock on the wall ticked steadily in the background filling the otherwise tranquil home, but the digital clock she could actually see read only 9:49.

Reaching for her phone, Claudia learned in the short time she'd been asleep, she missed one call from Tanner and two from Weston.

He left yet another voicemail expressing his need to apologize for how he'd spoken to her the other day. He knew Claudia was having a hard time with everything that was going on and wasn't sure how she'd react to him just showing up. But he knew he couldn't lose his wife *and* Claudia.

She called Weston back only to learn that he was already en route to her house and only a few minutes away. She cleaned up the mess she had made with Hope, then met him at the door.

There he stood. The moonlight reflected off his envy green-colored eyes as he smiled at her holding two dozen of the largest red roses imaginable. At first glance, Claudia smiled but then she noticed the flowers. She winced but tried to hide it with a smile. He tried to hand them to her, but she just stood entranced as her breathing shifted, hesitant to take them.

"I feel like red's not necessarily your fave, but I got them because they symbolize love... Claudia? Claudy."

"Yes," she said, snapping out of it, suddenly calming down. "Love. Thank you," she replied, slowly taking the bouquet from him, turning to walk down the hall toward the kitchen.

"I really want to apologize. I shouldn't have come at you like I did, knowing everything you've been dealing with. And I know you'd never do anything to intentionally hurt me."

Claudia leaned back onto the island and her rich hazel eyes full of fire and heat gazed at him intensely while he continued his apology.

"I want you to know I *did* go in and delete the footage. From everywhere," he quickly added, running his hands through his thick dark hair.

She tilted her head and her eyes lingered on his full lips as he spoke. "Hmm, good to know. And thank you... for the flowers. You're just a big ol' sweetie poo, huh West? This *must* be why I like you."

Weston gave a bashful grin, pleased that she seemed accepting of his apology.

Softly kissing his cheek, she whispered, "Give me a minute to change into something more suitable. Make yourself at home." With a sexy swing in her hips, she sauntered to the bedroom, knowing that his eyes were still on her.

Claudia removed what clothing she had on and confidently strode over to the dresser where she had to dig deep to find the lace cheeky panties and matching lace cami. She ran her fingers through her hair and threw it to the side, which made her look almost primal.

As she seductively emerged from her bedroom, he had just finished arranging the flowers in a vase he'd found. A vase he almost dropped when he took in her goddess-like perfection.

He immediately rushed over to her and ran his strong eager hands up her torso lifting her shirt. Kissing her stomach and working his way south, he began to slide her panties down fully intending to orally ease her distress.

"Not tonight," Claudia said as she slowly lifted his head back up to hers. "Fuck me. Right now," she whispered breathlessly in his ear before tearing off his dress shirt, sending buttons catapulting across the hardwood floor.

Her lips melted into his as she sucked his bottom lip into her mouth, biting it hard enough for him to flinch. He gasped through his teeth in pain, "Claudy, damn."

"Shut up. Don't call me that," she ordered as she pulled him back in and continued her aggressive embrace while hastily removing his clothes, leaving a trail from the kitchen to the bedroom.

He looked slightly confused when she pushed him back onto the bed, as she wasn't usually this assertive. His eyes wandered her body zealously as she seductively removed her crimson lace cami and slid down the matching panties over her thick muscular thighs. Weston was shocked to see how amazingly sexy that deep shade of red looked against her flawless caramel skin. Then he found himself wondering if he was wrong about her not liking the color. Delicate shades of pink or purple lingerie were usually her default.

Those thoughts quickly left his mind when, with swift cat-like precision, Claudia climbed up his body and landed her tender femininity down hard onto his manhood, as her French-manicured fingernails dug into his shoulders.

They both cried out, her in pleasure, he in unexpected pain that was able to be promptly disregarded because of how adeptly she was riding him, twirling and sliding her body up and down his massive length.

To regain the sexual dominance he was accustomed to having, he cupped her bottom and flipped her over onto her back while transitioning to a smooth, long, gentler stroke…

what he was accustomed to... how they often made love. His eyes widened when she smacked his ass, then dug her fingernails into his flesh to pull him deeper and harder inside of her. Guttural groans escaped her as she helped him fill her lady space as forcefully as possible.

"Stop this gentle shit and *fuck* me!"

She flipped him back over and resumed what had been pleasuring her so intensely. He laid there while she aggressively rode him with very little regard for his enjoyment or involvement, for that matter. The warm affectionate eye contact that was usually shared between them was non-existent. She seemed totally checked out.

He reached up to stroke her face to bring her gaze to his, "Claudy..."

Tilting her head back and shifting to avoid his touch, without any thought, she leaned in to put her hand over his mouth to stop him from saying whatever he was about to say and continued bucking and slamming her needy body onto his. He was basically her plaything at that moment, and he really wasn't sure how to feel about it. Any other man may have been thrilled to have a sexy curvy woman riding him with reckless abandon. Except, for Weston, it was more like his wife's selfish style of sex, which he didn't particularly enjoy.

As confused as he was, that didn't negate the fact that he was immersed so deep inside Claudia's tightness that he couldn't help but contribute to her feral moaning that was sure to awaken the neighbors – if she'd had any.

Claudia screamed out in Spanish while every muscle in her body clenched and convulsed as an orgasm loudly ripped through her trembling body. Out of breath, as her climax neared completion, he flipped her onto her back and continued driving into her with the same force that she delivered to him until he loudly finished as well.

Both breathing heavily and completely spent, he leaned in to tenderly kiss her. Instead, he was met with her fingers running through his thick salt and pepper hair while she used her other hand to push his body off hers. She turned over onto her side, away from him and immediately fell asleep.

Weston laid in Claudia's bed staring at the ceiling trying to figure out what the hell just happened.

*****

Claudia slowly roused to the smell of freshly brewed coffee. She emerged from her bedroom wearing only Weston's blue button-down dress shirt that she found on the floor. He observed her carefully as she took a seat at the island, her loose curls falling over her face that held a crooked smirk.

"How you feeling?" he asked tentatively, pouring coffee into her favorite Game of Thrones mug.

"Tired... Sore?" she replied as she winced and shifted in her seat. "What the hell happened last night?"

"You tell me," he said, walking around the island toward her. The unbuttoned shirt she was wearing was kept in place only by her petite but perky breasts. Weston ran his thumb down the area where there should have been buttons.

"Oh my gosh, where are the buttons? You ripped your shirt off?"

"No, *you* ripped my shirt off. And all the rest of my clothes for that matter."

Claudia's bottom jaw fell open and she could feel her cheeks begin to flush in embarrassment, "I am so sorry. I will replace this for you."

"Don't bother. It looks better on you, anyway," he said before hesitantly leaning in to give her a kiss. He was relieved when she accepted it and returned the affection after last night when she would barely let him even touch her.

"But you were definitely an animal last night, I've never seen you that... aggressive before. I was just trying to hold on and keep up," he admitted nervously.

Claudia remained silent, sipping her coffee as she worked to remember everything that happened. Dr. Pearce had specifically told her not to take that medication with alcohol, as it could have some less-than-desirable side effects. Was engaging in activities and not remembering one of them? She recalled taking the pill and then not really thinking twice about it when she drank that bottle of wine to de-stress. Next time she would certainly think twice about it, but she really didn't feel like explaining all of that to Weston. "I'm really sorry if I hurt you, West."

"It's okay. I'm a big boy," he smirked. "I can take it. But next time, maybe just one *glass* instead of one *bottle*?" he joked as he slid the empty wine bottle across the island toward her.

Weston walked with his coffee over to the sliding glass doors in the living room and looked out over the large grassy area that led into the thick woods. The misty fog was tinted orange by the burning sunrise to the left. His eyes scanned the infamous deck, which was the reason that he was even able to spend the night with Claudia for the first time. And then he realized, it was silly to blame the deck. He made his decisions that day, and every day he had spent with Claudia. Alessandra would not be missing him that morning, and if he was honest with himself, he didn't miss her that much either. Just not waking up to the boys is what yanked at his heartstrings.

"It's really beautiful here in the mornings." He turned back toward Claudia, "But you're beautiful-er."

"Oh yeah?" She bashfully giggled, "beautiful-errr, huh? I like it," she said before he leaned in and kissed her again.

"I see they never came to pick up that backhoe."

"No, I need to call them again, I guess. So what's on your agenda today?" she inquired, sipping her coffee.

"Ohh, I'm gonna go home and fight with my wife. She'll accuse me of being with you all night. I'll probably just deny it since everyone's in denial and she's still trying to pass that off as my baby."

"What? Even after you came clean about the vasectomy?"

"Crazy, right? I had my appointment and everything's still intact. Nothing's coming out of there that's not supposed to. Which is good because you definitely didn't give me time to put on a condom last night."

"Sorry," she repeated shamefully.

"What about you?"

"I'm taking a drive out to the prison with my new family," she answered sarcastically. "Isaiah had asked me to go see Miles. Something about wanting me to look into his eyes and see that he's innocent."

"You know you don't have to do that, right? You don't owe either of them anything."

"I know. It's been like thirty years of him trying to contact me. I *will* say he's definitely held steadfast, maintaining his innocence the entire time," she said, sipping more coffee. "I'm only going because... I guess I would like to develop a relationship with my brother, and I don't honestly think it will or can happen unless I do this. But it's fine," Claudia said resolutely. "I'll hear him out, remind him of the evidence at hand, and hope that Isaiah finally sees him for the real murderer he is."

"Okay, well just be safe. Upside, there are cameras all over the place in there, so if he tries anything out of pocket..."

The thought of that made Claudia shudder and sigh. "I'm just nervous."

Weston nodded, "I have a remedy for that," he said, sliding open his dress shirt and gazing over her beautiful nude body.

She pulled it closed and went to button it but had already quickly forgotten how she'd destroyed that poor man's shirt. "I'm sorry," she said regretfully. "I just can't right now."

He gave her a sad face, dramatically poking out his bottom lip like his sons do when they want their way.

Claudia rolled her eyes and smiled. "It's just that... everything is still really... sore," she replied, shifting in her seat again.

"Well, you know what daddy is supposed to do when you have a boo-boo, right?" he whispered seductively into her ear.

Before she could utter an answer, he had hoisted her up onto the marble-top island, smacked the side of her ass, and began to shower her special place with kisses to make it all better. He would continue to do so until she screamed and desperately begged him to stop the torturous pleasure.

26

The three-hour ride to the prison with Isaiah was so incredibly awkward that Claudia began to wonder if it was such a good idea. Maybe she should have gone alone to have this discussion with Miles. Though they were trying to get to know one another, the conversation with her newfound brother didn't flow so easily and was filled with many uncomfortable silences. They didn't seem to have much in common other than the same mother. It made Claudia wonder, had they been raised together, would they have been more similar?

As they pulled up to the austere concrete structure with barred windows surrounded by angry fencing, Claudia began to feel queasy. She removed both of the firearms she had concealed on her body and placed them inside the glove box.

"My gosh, how many guns do you need? You're not even on duty right now."

"Look, it's better to have 'em and not need 'em," she replied as she locked the glove box.

After making it through the metal detector, the drug dogs, hair/body check, and sign-in process, they finally arrived at the family visitation area. Guests of inmates filed into the large open room full of plain metal tables and chairs bolted to the ground. As they made their way to an available table, Claudia noticed how many cameras had eyes on her. Even in her line of work, she wasn't much of a fan of being surveilled, which is why it took a stalker for her to even consider installing cameras. There were also multiple correctional officers, armed with Tasers, strategically placed around the room and outside of it.

"Thank you so much for agreeing to come. I feel like once you talk to him, you'll see that he couldn't have done it. Like, I really believe that."

Claudia simply didn't respond as they took a seat at a table on the far side of the room. It was one of the larger tables that probably should have been used for a more substantial group, but Claudia had no desire to sit that close to the man who she knew murdered her mother.

Her stomach was in knots, wondering what she was supposed to say to him after three decades. After all, she was the reason he was there. Would he have killed her too the night he escaped from the officer's grasp and lunged at her in the police station? He basically harassed and threatened her for years and she was finally about to have her first verbal exchange with him as an adult.

Claudia's stomach churned and she felt an overwhelming need to vomit, but she held her breath until it started to subside.

"I don't think this is a good idea."

Just as she stood up to make a quick getaway, the inmates began to file into the room, so she re-claimed her seat and breathed deeply to calm herself down.

She watched as the families greeted the inmates so happily, knowing that *their* family reunion would not be one of such pleasure. The mere idea of him even attempting to embrace her made the initial queasiness return even stronger.

A few moments had passed and everyone seemed to have entered the room, except there was still no Miles. Claudia leaned onto the table resting her head in her hands, thinking that now would definitely be the perfect time to escape. But she was too late, again. She really just needed to start going with her gut.

Miles stopped at the entryway and scanned the room looking for his family. With her head still down, Claudia shifted her eyes up and watched indifferently through her fingers as he strolled across the room toward them. Her breathing slowed as she listened to his footsteps. It felt like all other sounds in the room dissipated and all she could see and hear were Miles and her own breathing. As her eyes made their way up his body, his feet, his gait, his large rough hands, and sturdy body... Claudia continued her slow breaths as she watched the smile form across his face. That smile. He greeted his son with a warm but masculine handshake and embrace. But that *smile*...

As the two men stood staring down at her and the sound abruptly returned, Claudia immediately jumped up and backed away breathing heavily, drawing the attention of the guards and other visitors. She could feel her heart skip beats and her skin instantly moisten.

"It's you," she whispered, grasping her hip desperately for her missing firearm.

There she was, now wide awake, yet still defenseless. The man whose face she could never see in her nightmares was standing before her like nothing ever happened. But it had. Watching him walk across the room snatched her back to her six-year-old self, trying to feign sleep in hopes that it would deter him from coming into her room in the middle of the night. But it never did. Her years of nightmares weren't simply a product of an overactive imagination; they were horrific memories. Those creaky floorboards in the hallway outside of her childhood room. The door slowly opening. His dirty work boots walking across her floor. His musty smell of alcohol and cigarettes. Her fear. His abrasive painful touch. It was all *real*.

"Claudia, please-" Miles begged quietly.

"It was *you!*" she yelled, breathing deeply, still retreating until she backed into the guard who was approaching behind her. "I was just a *child!* But I *remember* now," she panted, her face full of angst and disgust. "Our secret? You coming into my room... *what you did to me*? I *begged* for you to stop... e-ve-ry time."

"Please, Claudia, I didn't-"

"You *did*, you sick fuck!"

"Shhhh..." Miles whispered, "Please, you can't say that in here."

"Why not? Because it's *true*?" she vented even louder.

They were surrounded by correctional officers and poor Isaiah held a look of dismay on his face, eyes shifting back and forth between the two of them as they had their heated exchange. He was unsure of whom to believe, as he wanted so desperately to have his father in his life and believe that he was a good and innocent man. However, Claudia's visceral savage reaction to simply seeing him added so much tension to the room, that it was hard not to believe her.

She instinctively reached for her weapon again and Isaiah truly believed that had she had access to it, she would've shot his father.

"It's not true," he stammered. "You're just... you're remembering it wrong."

This man who did the most heinous things to her as a small child was standing before this group gaslighting her and all she wanted to do was rip out his throat. Claudia screamed and aggressively lunged toward him when she was restrained from behind by a C.O. yelling at her to calm down. One stepped in front of Miles as well to prevent a physical altercation.

Claudia closed her eyes, took deep but erratic breaths, then stared into his tainted soul with pure hatred. Forcefully shaking herself free of the guard's grasp, she took a single step forward. "*I'm* misremembering, huh?" she asked calmly. "Am I also misremembering the mole at the base of your penis that my tiny fingers used to graze over?"

Silence thundered through that visitation room with not even a breath to be heard, as all eyes were on the three of them. "Why don't you *show* us?" she whispered.

Miles' eyes widened and immediately shifted down to his crotch, then back to Claudia, which Isaiah promptly took as an admission of guilt. "That... I- It wasn't supposed to happen like that," he whispered. "You gotta believe me. Can we *please* talk about this privately?" As quiet as that room was, he might as well have stood on the table and made a proclamation.

"Seems you've had enough *private* time with me. But thank you! For basically admitting your sexual deviance, you lecherous pig."

"No! No, no, that's not what I meant! I-"

Claudia turned toward the C.O. "How about when you lock him back up, you throw away the *fucking* key this time."

She walked toward the exit knowing that her work had been done. There were at least twenty inmates in that room who witnessed that entire exchange.

As Claudia passed by and made eye contact with a massive blue-eyed man with tattoos covering the entire right side of his head, this stranger turned his mouth down in disgust and gave her a subtle nod. She smirked and returned the motion. It was common knowledge how inmates felt about child abusers. Miles was about to find out firsthand.

The car ride to the prison was nothing compared to the unease on the ride back. Isaiah quietly stared out the window completely distraught, all his boyhood dreams of having his father in his life, shattered before he could even say hello.

"I know what Miles meant to you, and I'm sorry you had to see that," Claudia sincerely expressed.

"I'm sorry he... did that to you," Isaiah replied timidly. A few moments passed before he spoke again, "They're going to hurt him aren't they." It wasn't really a question, as he already knew the answer.

"Absolutely," Claudia replied with no remorse as they completed the long drive home in total silence.

*****

Claudia had so much to say, but nothing at all as she sat stoically in her usual spot across from Dr. Pearce. She literally didn't even know where to begin after coming to the realization that her stepfather had violated her. She wasn't sure how it was even possible to forget all of that. But now that the memories were brought forward, Claudia recalled everything and was able to expound in great detail, her nightmares that were actually long-repressed memories. She realized that was also the reason her childhood therapist went missing from her recollection, as well. She had blocked out everything that had to do with the pain Miles had inflicted.

Dr. Pearce had suspected the trauma she was experiencing in her dreams could be mirroring actual events of past sexual misconduct. She just wasn't sure by whom and was hesitant to broach the topic given everything else Claudia had been dealing with. She didn't want to add additional trauma to confront, at least until they got some of the other issues under control. But this information definitely explained so much, such as Claudia's overall hypersexuality. While yes, Claudia was single and free to mingle with whomever, wherever she pleased, she hadn't been making the best decisions on the whom, in addition to the where. Very often, she expressed that it was just emotionless sex to obtain the ultimate exhilarating end release. It was happening with colleagues and occasionally in risky locations that could potentially jeopardize her career, not to mention her highly sexualized fantasies and arousal at inappropriate times.

"I'm not a sex addict Dr. Pearce," she said with a tone in response to their conversation.

"That's not what I said-"

"Well, that's what it *feels* like you said," Claudia interrupted.

"Hypersexuality is not sex addiction, but more a side effect of, or reaction to, past trauma. Some people who have experienced this type of abuse will withdraw from sexual activity altogether, whereas others, like yourself, drift to the other end of the spectrum, possibly using it as a method to reclaim control over your sexuality. And there's nothing wrong with wanting control over a part of your life that had been under someone else's command before you were even old enough to consent. But that control needs to be taken in a healthy manner that doesn't put you, your livelihood, or others at risk."

Claudia nodded, even though she still felt like she was being called a slut.

She talked to Dr. Pearce about when she finally got up the nerve to tell her mother that Miles was coming to her room at night. Claudia was told to "stop saying things like that." In addition to the inexplicable love Janet had for her abusive husband, their financial situation compelled her mother to stay with him and when she ended up pregnant, that just made it worse for Claudia. She didn't understand it at the time, but the further the pregnancy progressed, the more frequent the midnight visits became to Claudia's room.

"As an officer, I see firsthand how difficult it can often be to escape an abusive relationship, but as a child, all I knew was that she was my mother. She was supposed to keep me *safe*," Claudia moaned with a heavy sigh. "But she couldn't even keep herself safe," Claudia painfully reminisced, looking off through the window across the room. "He had the audacity to say it was all a mistake. But you don't mistakenly beat your wife and touch her child."

As Dr. Pearce was about to respond, Claudia stood up and walked over to the window. So she remained quiet to allow her patient to process.

"I didn't want to lose my mother, but... I feel like a horrible person for thinking that I'm almost glad it happened. Am I?" she asked, looking to Dr. Pearce through moist hazel eyes. "A horrible person?"

"Absolutely not. You were a child literally trapped in a hellish situation. Your mother didn't listen to you when you came forward, and it didn't seem like she was going to leave on her own. So her death, while tragic and untimely, was what got you out of that house and away from your abuser. Feeling a sense of relief about getting out of that situation does not make you a bad person."

Claudia nodded, "But what about the fact that through all of this... all the disgusting things I've told you, as I stand here, all I can think about is sex with Weston."

"Also does not make you a bad person. You're feeling bad right now, and the reality of the situation is... well... not to make light of things but orgasms just make you feel better. Especially when the person providing them also makes you feel safe and loved."

Claudia was on the verge of shedding tears but laughter replaced them because she wasn't expecting to hear that from her therapist.

"Whaaat!? They do!" Dr. Pearce continued. "All that dopamine and endorphins - those are the *official* feel-good chemicals! And from what you've expressed to me, Weston's been giving you *multiple* episodes of... feel-good chemicals."

Claudia continued to chuckle at how her doctor turned this guilty-feeling sex talk into something medical while dabbing the slight moisture from her eyes.

Dr. Pearce walked over to Claudia at the expansive window. "Look, if you're ok with this, the goal of our treatment can shift to helping you manage those urges and lessen your extreme behaviors so you can maintain *healthy* sexual activities. How's that sound?"

"Like work," Claudia replied with a small smile, but comfortable in the fact that maybe she could truly begin the healing process.

27

Detective Tanner Lockhart's eyes were getting heavy from combing through the low-resolution video footage. There had to be *something* that they were missing. There's simply no way any one person could avoid every single camera, every time. What was the catch?

"What are you doing over there, Lockhart? You tryin' to get Rookie of the Year or something? You know that's not a thing in police work, right? Go home!" Burgess shouted across the room.

Tanner laughed. "Yeah, I know. Just looking through this Science Center footage that just came in a bit ago. I'll be headin' out soon. Be safe out there!"

He squeezed his eyes shut for a few seconds before refocusing on the raw footage. He immediately sprung to life when he saw something peculiar in the upper right-hand corner of the video.

The time stamp read 7:57 p.m. just before the Science Center closed for that night. They were open later than usual for a district science competition. While the other children were running around the exhibits engrossed in their activities, while parents and teachers socialized with each other, barely supervising those children, there was one older youth who appeared to be standing near the emergency stairwell talking to someone off-camera.

This child was visiting the Science Center with a group of children who were all wearing royal blue Polo shirts, most of whom also donned matching face masks, making any facial recognition nearly impossible. As Tanner zoomed in, the footage got much grainier but then he saw it. A black gloved hand came into the frame handing over an item, much like the gloved hand that passed off the bag of body parts in the other video. He continued to watch as the child stuffed money into his back pocket, looked around, then walked away.

He rushed to pull up the alley footage sent from the Westin Hotel and quickly scrolled through that. "Ohhhh shit! Fuck!" he hissed, pounding his fist onto his desk. "FUCK!"

Tanner immediately looked around the squad room and there was no one else there who was on that case. With the perfect opportunity to get rid of this evidence, he grabbed the flash drive from his desk, logged out, then logged back in as Detective Eric Burgess using the password he recalled overseeing him type in once. He quickly moved the incriminating Science Center clips onto the device, ensuring they were no longer accessible to his colleagues on the department's private drive.

Grabbing his jacket and car keys, Tanner ejected the device, stuffed it in his pocket, and immediately shot out of the squad room.

*****

Claudia stepped out of the bathroom wrapped in a plush peach towel with her loose curls up in a messy bun. As she applied coconut oil to her damp bronze skin, she noticed another bruise forming on her right shoulder. She could only assume that it must have happened when the correctional officer grabbed her the other day. Playing back the events in her mind as she continued to get dressed, a small smile formed across her face as she thought about how Miles was beaten to near death after her visit. One thing inmates definitely frown upon is touching small children. Once they heard that, it was almost like a Pavlovian response to come running and whoop his ass.

Claudia looked herself over in the mirror, though there was nothing extravagant to see there. It was just going to be her on the couch with a glass of wine, a bowl of popcorn, and a movie. So she was only wearing the Pittsburgh Marathon t-shirt Weston had left at her house and a pair of lavender lace panties. *One day I'm gonna buy myself some tits large enough to require a bra*, she thought to herself.

Claudia jumped when she heard a car skid to a stop in her gravel driveway, so she grabbed a pair of shorts to throw on. Immediately looking around for her phone to open the camera app, she remembered that it was in the living room on the charger. "Shit!"

As she made her way to it, her heart pounded heavier when she heard the unexpected visitor banging loudly on her front door. She tiptoed barefoot over to the end table to collect her .38 caliber pistol that was hidden beneath, then made her way to the door as the banging continued.

When she peeked out and saw that it was only Tanner, she heaved a sigh of relief and slid her gun into the back waistband of her shorts.

Unlocking the door, as soon as she turned the knob, Tanner pushed his way in and headed briskly down her entryway, breathing heavily.

"What's wrong? What are you doing here?" She asked, shutting the door and then following him into her kitchen.

"They sent the Science Center surveillance video over this evening," he said, looking around to make sure they were alone.

"Okay, that's great. We can start going through it tomorrow."

"I already started, Claudia. I found it! I know now!"

Claudia frowned in confusion, "What are you talking about?"

"No! Don't give me that doe-eyed innocent look!" he yelled, coming closer to her. "Tell me what the *fuck* is going on!"

Claudia stood breathing heavily, startled as Tanner yelled down at her.

"This!" he screamed as he grabbed her right arm and twisted it so her forearm was facing up, revealing a black Mayan tattoo that extended the length of her entire inner forearm.

"If you want to murder the people, Claudia, wear. A longer. *Hoodie!*"

Her heart still pounded in her ears, "I don't... I- That wasn't *me!*"

"Stop it!" Tanner interrupted. "Don't even try to explain that shit away. The video showed *your arm*! When you handed that ear off, your sleeve slid up just enough to reveal the bottom part of *this* tattoo on your wrist!" he yelled, forcefully grabbing her arm again. "You finally slipped up."

"No! No, no... that's not right," she muttered, squeezing her eyes shut. "We're cops! We *help* people!"

"Is this why you wear long sleeves all the time? Even in the summer? No one at work even *knows* about this tattoo, do they? But *I've* seen you naked. *I* know," he whispered unnervingly in her ear.

Tanner had her tightly backed up against the refrigerator hurling questions and accusations, wanting to know how and why.

"You think they wouldn't eventually match it to the handoff in the alley? The *alley*... Oh my gah - you killed that homeless man too, didn't you?" he asked in shock with his hands on his head.

Still breathing erratically and shaking her head, Claudia whispered, "No... no... no," as a tear slowly rolled down her cheek. "Why would you *say* that!?"

"Don't cry. No one has to know, Claudia." Tanner wiped the moisture away with his thumb and slid her one dangling curl out of her face as he stood over her breathing deeply. Claudia froze. That one simple gesture that Miles used to do every time he visited her room thrust her right back to her painful childhood.

"I erased it from the drive. I have the only copy," he whispered forebodingly. "And as long as you agree to give me what I want..." She squeezed her eyes shut as his hand slipped down the front of her body fondling her right breast, before sliding down her stomach. She didn't want his hands on her, but just like when she was a child, she felt paralyzed to stop it, even though she was no longer defenseless.

"I *help* people," she whispered, still shaking her head and struggling for breath.

As though he were trying to convince her of it, "We *both* know you did it," he murmured, sliding his fingers between her legs. "But ya know, you could have just told me. I could have *helped* you help the people. I *love* that you were taking out the trash, cleaning up our streets. It was actually quite brilliant," he moaned while continuing to manipulate her femininity with his invasive fingers.

Claudia's jagged breathing slowed and began to level out. The fear began to subside learning that he wasn't there to arrest her, but with an offer to *assist*. As she opened her eyes and looked up to sharply meet Tanner's heated gaze, a sense of calm, among other inappropriate feelings, suddenly washed over her body.

"Really?" she asked curiously.

"Absolutely," he growled while continuing to massage her. She began to slowly gyrate her pelvis to the rhythm of his digits while staring deeply into his bright eyes. "I love how the idea of that turns you on so much," he said as she began assertively moving forward, backing him toward the living room.

"It does," she said as she flirtatiously pushed him backward and offered a seductive smile. Oddly, Claudia looked so different to him... darker. She seemed to exude this glow of sexual confidence all of a sudden... Almost feral... It was erotic.

"But, guess what?" she asked slyly, glancing down toward the bulge in his pants, licking her lips.

"What?" he asked in a haze of arousal.

The seductive smile immediately faded from her face, "Two can't keep a secret." She whipped her gun out from behind her and shot him in the thigh.

Tanner hit the living room floor, clutching his leg, screaming in pain. He pulled the blanket that was dangling off the nearby chair and used it to apply pressure to stop the bleeding.

"Claudia! You *bitch*!" He screamed out, rooting around for his cell phone.

Staring down at him, she pointed the gun at his head, "Give me. The fucking phone."

He fearfully complied, slowly handing it up to her.

"And stop. Calling me. *CLAUDIA!* Why doesn't anyone see *me*? They only see *fucking* Claudia. That bitch is *weak*. Everything you stupid little boys admire about her, *I'm* the reason! *I'm* the confidence and sex appeal!"

Tanner's eyes widened while he listened to her in confusion. "Who *are* you?" he stuttered.

"I'm Ruby. *I'm* the one who rode you like the Kentucky Derby in your police cruiser. You think Claudia would ever be that adventurous? You think she would ever risk her career by having sex with a... *rookie*?" she asked with disdain.

Tanner was still breathing heavily in shock, trying to figure out an escape from this mess he was in.

"Ruby. Okay, I got it. *I* see you," he said nervously, clearly trying to placate her. "Can we call 9-1-1?" he asked slowly, "Please?"

"Why would we do that? Oh, you think you're leaving here alive? That's so adorable," she said mockingly. "Wait, are you *crying* right now? Funny how you just turned into a little bitch all of a sudden when just five minutes ago, you barged up in here ready to *take* what Claudia wasn't willing to give you in *our kitchen*! Blackmail simply doesn't suit you, Tanner."

Ruby paced the living room. "Just like Miles," she spewed with hatred in her voice. "Do you have any idea how many times he put his hands on Claudia, just like you did? *Un*wanted. *Un*invited. Claudia couldn't defend herself against such a formidable oppressor, so *I* came to assist. Just like I'm here *now* to fix shit. Hey, call me Viola Davis, why don'tcha – seems like I'm just The *fucking* Help!" Ruby screamed. "But it's fine because I get shit *done*."

Ruby pulled up one of the wooden dining room chairs and sat in front of Tanner with her legs open and her elbows on her knees in a very relaxed, but masculine position. "You know Miles is innocent, right?" she asked with a satisfied smile. "Aaaaghhhh," she yelled, "I've been waiting forever to get that out! *I* killed that tramp, Janet."

Tanner's eyes widened even more. "You killed your mother?"

"I killed *Claudia's* mother," she replied with an air of satisfaction. "It was genius. She was so pregnant. She couldn't carry the laundry basket up the stairs, so she always kneeled over it to put her weight on it as she moved it up a few steps at a time. Once she made it to the top, still hunched over, I used what little weight I had to force my hands into her shoulders and pushed her backward down the steps. It was perfect. Miles was sent away, I no longer had to deal with Claudia's trash mother who didn't believe Miles could ever touch her, and we got a new family. A *decent* family. Except for that fucking dog. But it's okay. I took care of him too."

Ruby stood up and stretched, "Man, this is so much better than therapy. Way more cathartic. I hear Dr. Pearce is one amazing bitch, but we just can't tell her these things because she'll think we're crazy."

"You *are* crazy," he mumbled under his shallow breath.

"Wait, hold the hell up! Wasn't your dick just hard as advanced calculus while offering to *help* me? Doesn't that make *you* crazi-errr? Because *I* feel like I've developed a pretty just system here. I *helped* those children. Every time one of those men would hit, punch, verbally denigrate them... Every unwanted touch..." Ruby continued pacing. "Every tear shed as a result of such things... it eats away at you! It destroys a child piece by piece! Those men took pieces of those children, so I took pieces of *them*."

"But you said your biological father never hurt you..." Ruby shot him a sharp look. "I mean Claudia said... She told me that herself."

"He didn't. He left her to fall prey to a sexual predator then went off and created a whole new family. She had to live her life without her father, so it was only *fair* that he got to live his life without his daughter. So I killed that bitch Teena, too. Made a few little adjustments to that airbag situation and ran that little whore right off the road. See? A *just* system. An eye for an eye." Ruby said casually, circling Tanner like a voracious shark. "Slicing up her bio dad was just the icing. We won't miss him," she said, shaking her head dramatically.

Ruby kneeled in front of Claudia's wounded colleague, "So what did you do with the video, Tanner?"

"I'll tell you if you let me call 9-1-1, please," he pleaded.

"You'll tell me because I *asked*, and if you don't, I'll blow your brains all over this plush Safavieh rug, and have Pier One deliver me a new one by Wednesday," she replied casually.

"I deleted them from the main server."

"And where's the copy?"

"In my pocket," he replied with even more shallow breaths as he retrieved it for her. "It's the only one."

"Are you lying?"

"No! I swear!"

"Good. Ya know, we have a lot in common! I deleted some footage too. Canvassing my father's neighborhood was close," she nodded, re-claiming her seat in the wooden chair. "That old lady caught me on her camera walking by. Only by sheer luck was Claudia the one who visited her to check her footage, otherwise, I would've been noticed back then. Just messy... I should've used that messenger service again..."

"So *you* were the one stalking Claudia?" he asked as his breathing became increasingly labored. He wasn't going to make it much longer. She would need to kill him so his official cause of death would fit her narrative.

"If Claudia were the victim, then she couldn't be your unsub. It was simply a diversion to cast suspicion elsewhere... and, well, it was just fun. I got cupcakes out of the deal," Ruby said as she stepped away from Tanner. "But it's okay because as far as they'll be concerned Detective Lockhart, *you* were stalking Claudia." Then she turned and shot him twice in the chest.

Once his upper body fell back onto the floor, she checked for a pulse. Then her attention shifted to the item in her other hand.

Fuck. This damn phone. They're gonna know he was here. Think... THINK, Ruby!

After deleting his and Claudia's call and text history, she wiped the phone down, put his prints back on it, then used his hand to stuff it back into his pocket. Ruby immediately grabbed her phone and began an Oscar-worthy performance hyperventilating and crying before the phone even started ringing.

"9-1-1, what's your emer-"

"He's in my house! I- ...Detective Claudi- aaaagh!!! Noooo!! No *pleeease!*" She continued pleading while muffling the phone, then disconnected the call. They could trace it and now knowing she's a detective, it would absolutely lead to a much faster arrival time. So she figured with her rural location, she had about twelve to fifteen minutes, tops.

She immediately slinked out of her lace panties, wrapped Tanner's large hand around them, rubbed them on his nose and mouth, then shoved them into his front pants pocket. After grabbing another pair to put on, Ruby ran into the kitchen, grabbed a knife from the holder, then forcefully slammed the back of her body against her stainless steel side-by-side refrigerator. The cereal containers that sat atop the appliance hit her head and spilled open before they landed spattering Special-K and Raisin Bran all through her hair and across the floor, where she then dropped the knife. She ran through the cereal on the floor crushing it and tracking it into the living room.

Resuming act two of her performance, she finally answered Lainey's sixth back-to-back call since officers were dispatched to her residence.

In faux tears, Claudia began, "He's dead! I- I shot him! I didn't *mean* to but-" she said between sobs. "He came to my house banging on my door... he- he was so... angry!"

"Who!? Are you ok!?"

"It was Tanner! You were right!" Ruby cried softly.

"It's okay, we're coming," Lainey said. "Just stay where you are."

As quickly as the call ended, Ruby's tears turned off like a light switch. She grabbed a pair of the black nitrile gloves and swiftly collected the bloody blanket to hide so she could burn it later, then headed to her bedroom to locate a hidden Ziploc baggie full of seemingly random items. After bringing the contents out to Tanner to transfer additional DNA, she slid on a pair of shoes and snuck out the back toward his car to leave more gifts there. While in his trunk,

Ruby noticed a set of four bungee cords that Tanner likely used to secure items onto his motorcycle. *This is too fucking perfect.* She grabbed one and ran back into the house.

Several times she wrapped the bungee cord around her neck and began to choke herself to the point that she was barely able to breathe. While she assumed that Tanner's DNA would be on them, she was not taking any chances. So she put the ends of the cord in his hands and pulled it back and forth just to make sure his epithelial cells were there, then she dropped it a few feet from his body.

Her eyes darted over to the fish across the room. "Sorry Joffrey," she said coldly before shattering the aquarium onto the floor, sending water splashing everywhere. She winced as she purposefully stepped on some of the glass.

Ruby screamed violently as she smashed the 52-inch flat screen against the wall then pulled it to the floor, shattered the standing lamp, then slightly displaced much of the furniture.

She took a deep breath before smashing the side of her head into the concrete mantel, consciously dripping the blood all over the floor, then strategically walking through it. She threw her body down onto her couch several times in different positions then looked down at Tanner. Ruby bent his knees so his feet were flat on the ground, then stood over him to drip blood downward on top of the shoes. She even went as far as pressing cereal into the grooves of the soles of his shoes.

She kneeled beside Tanner and used his left hand to grab her hair and scratch the right side of her face. She violently scratched him up as well, leaving their blood and

DNA all over each other. His shirt was lightly ripped and untucked so that he looked like he was involved in a violent physical struggle with her.

Ruby saw the lights from the police cruisers approaching her house, so she took her position.

Lainey was first through the door, announcing herself with her weapon drawn, just in case. She crept down the short dark entryway and was caught off guard when cereal crunched beneath her feet in the kitchen. Slowly peering around the corner to the right, she saw Detective Tanner Lockhart on the floor and she motioned for the officers behind her to tend to him. She continued scanning the room to finally find her partner in the far left dark corner, rocking back and forth in tears holding the gun.

"Claudia, honey, it's me, Lainey," she said, slowly approaching her while holstering her firearm. "You're safe now. Can you put your weapon down?"

Ruby looked up at Claudia's partner and set the gun down gently. Lainey ran over to her, dropped to her knees, and painfully took in Claudia's bruised and bloodied face, torn clothing, and trembling blood-stained hands. Normally so composed, Lainey just didn't know what else to do other than wrap her traumatized friend in her arms and tell her it would be okay. Ruby frigidly stared across the room while in Lainey's embrace as police and EMTs invaded her home, eerily similar to how it happened thirty years ago.

epilogue

One month later

Turns out Weston's profile wasn't so wrong after all, as far as the department knew. They'd found the man who had been stalking Detective Martinez, following her domestic cases, then subsequently murdering the men affiliated with them. Lainey was right. It *was* an inside job. They just had the wrong insider. But that was neither here nor there.

As far as the evidence presented, when police searched Tanner Lockhart's personal vehicle, they found a receipt for Gigi's Cupcakes stashed between the center console and the driver's side seat. In the glove box was a single loose key that matched the keys Claudia had before she changed her locks. In his trunk were not only the three other bungee cords that matched the one Tanner used to choke Claudia but also hidden in the side compartment was Dr. Walker's Tag Heuer engraved watch and Clem Rossi's wedding band that they didn't even know was missing. To ice this beautifully made cake, his prints and epithelial cells were all over every piece of evidence they found, including Claudia's panties they found in his front pocket. He must've stolen them the night he killed her fish, was the theory.

Video footage confirmed Lainey's testimony that Tanner mentioned being at the Science Center with his niece the week prior to the ear being discovered. It was suggested that he was there to case the location before leaving the body part. Lainey, along with the rest of the squad, also recalled how he was so content to simply, in his own words, "Let it go."

Add to that the video footage of him running from his car and violently banging on Claudia's front door. It simply helped confirm the story Claudia spoon-fed them about Tanner barging his way into her house and forcing himself on her in the kitchen, where she tried to defend herself with the knife. He knocked it out of her hand before dragging her into the living room by her hair, which just happened to be full of cereal residue. There, she fought off his brutal attack and was able to make it to her weapon that was affixed to the underside of the end table. With her vision blurry from the head trauma, still struggling to catch her breath, she fired once hitting Tanner in the thigh, then two shots center mass.

The very next night, a fire was lit in remembrance of Tanner Lockhart so she could burn the blood-stained blanket and the flash drive that incriminated her. The upside to them knowing she killed him was this time she didn't need to bury a body. Little did anyone know that beyond those beautiful trees, deeper into the woods on Claudia's property, Ruby had used that backhoe to lay eleven other abusive men to rest. She'd only recently decided to put them on display for her own personal delight.

Lainey watched Detective Martinez step out of her car, but there was something different about her. The curly ponytail she often wore had been transitioned to long, straight, blown-out hair. "Welcome back! And look at *youuu*! I knew you'd look phenomenal in red! Where are you going?"

The detective flipped her hair, smirked, and nodded a subtle thank you. Of course, she looked phenomenal - she always had.

"Same place you're going. Coffee and work. I just wanted to look good on my first day back."

Levar immediately noticed her when she walked through the Steamy Bean doors. He always had, but this time was different. Claudia had always been sexy-cute with her fresh face and curly locks, but today she was sexy-hot with reddish lips and smoky eye makeup that emphasized their hazel color. Her gaze even looked sharper... Deeper... Focused... More intense. She was moving with excess confidence and energy as she approached the counter. Normally, Levar would have been preparing her regular coffee order, but he was so entranced by her that he couldn't move.

"Welcome to the Steamy Bean. How can I help you?" the cashier asked.

Ruby bent down to look in the glass case, smoothed her fallen hair behind her left ear, and said, "I'll have a medium coffee. Black... And that red velvet cupcake."

THE END

If you've enjoyed my first psychological thriller, your reviews on Amazon and Goodreads are incredibly helpful to authors. Please and thank you!

More from J.R. Mason:
The Confessions Series:
Confessions of a Sane Single Woman
Soulmate Setbacks: Confessions II

Acknowledgments

So many people contributed medical, random, weird, and/or disturbing information that helped this creation to be more accurate and authentic. Thus, I would like to extend a heartfelt thank you to Lieutenant William Ahlgren, Detective Justin Hewitt, Officer Garrett Kimmell, Laura McMullen, M.D., Keith Duncan, Ph.D., M.D., Joshua Sckolnick, M.D., Deah Washington, M.A., L.P.C., Moses Cox, Anthony Schneider, Mark Hoag, Edward Azeem, Phyllis Williams, Jocelyn Bol, Levar Bundridge, and Triara Mason.

You all can thank my mother for Tanner's death lol... She said, "Name him Tanner. She should sleep with him, then kill him." Okay, Mom. You got it!

My irreplaceable friends Kimberly, Heather, Jennifer, Ellise, Crystal, Michael, and Kathryn, were all on hand with thoughts, ideas, beta reading, or simply readily available to listen to me vent. Your input and excitement for this story were concerning, but appreciated lol...

To my readers, thank you so much for having enough faith in me as I attempted this genre switch. You have no idea how nervous I was throughout this entire process. I appreciate your support!

The entire Instagram author community who is so incredibly supportive with their many words of wisdom and encouragement (along with answers to my many, *many* bookish questions), particularly Emerald O'Brien and L.C. Son.

About the Author

J.R. Mason first dipped her toes into the writing pool when she published her nonfiction Confessions Series, a self-described bad romance – *Confessions of a Sane Single Woman* and *Soulmate Setbacks: Confessions II*. Though a third Confessions book was requested, J.R. couldn't pull herself away from her dark desire to delve into a suspenseful fiction project.

Mason received her Bachelor of Arts in Journalism and Mass Communication from Cleveland State University and her Master of Arts in Advertising / Graphic Design / Public Relations from Point Park University. A full-time marketing specialist position, along with running a freelance design company keeps her quite busy, leaving little free time for her guilty pleasures – movies and massages!

This Ambridge, PA native also takes joy in playing her trumpet, kayaking, screenplay writing, travel, outdoor fires on cool nights (but not to burn people's possessions), anything with real sugar in it, and reading erotica or psychological thrillers.

Keep up with J.R.'s latest releases:
jrenecreative.com/books
Follow me on IG: author_j.r.mason

CPSIA information can be obtained
at www.ICGtesting.com
Printed in the USA
LVHW060928070623
749110LV00033B/183